D0056975

ALSO BY LYNN STEGER STRONG

Hold Still

WANT

WANT

a novel

Lynn Steger Strong

HENRY HOLT AND COMPANY NEW YORK

Henry Holt and Company
Publishers since 1866
120 Broadway
New York, New York 10271
www.henryholt.com

Henry Holt® and ® are registered trademarks of
Macmillan Publishing Group, LLC.

Copyright © 2020 by Lynn Steger Strong
All rights reserved.
Distributed in Canada by Raincoast Book Distribution Limited

Library of Congress Cataloging-in-Publication Data

Names: Strong, Lynn Steger, 1983– author.
Title: Want : a novel / Lynn Steger Strong.
Description: First edition. | New York, New York : Henry Holt and Company, 2020.
Identifiers: LCCN 2019040523 (print) | LCCN 2019040524 (ebook) | ISBN 9781250247544 (hardcover) | ISBN 9781250247537 (ebook)
Classification: LCC PS3619.T7785 W36 2020 (print) | LCC PS3619.T7785 (ebook) | DDC 813/.6—dc23
LC record available at https://lccn.loc.gov/2019040523
LC ebook record available at https://lccn.loc.gov/2019040524

Our books may be purchased in bulk for promotional, educational, or business use. Please contact your local bookseller or the Macmillan Corporate and Premium Sales Department at (800) 221-7945, extension 5442, or by email at MacmillanSpecialMarkets@macmillan.com.

First Edition 2020

Designed by Kelly S. Too

Printed in the United States of America

1 3 5 7 9 10 8 6 4 2

This is a work of fiction. As is true in many fictional works, aspects of the story were inspired by life experiences. No identification with actual, real life persons or events is intended, nor should any such identification be inferred.

For Peter, Isabel, and Luisa

WANT

2000

I'M SIXTEEN AND Sasha's seventeen and we go out to the beach at night and no one's there. We've thrown a party at her house and I have fallen, scraped my knee, getting a piggyback ride from a boy I know only offered it to me to impress her.

You tired, runner girl? he said.

They all call me runner girl.

We've freed ourselves of all the other people. We've gotten drunk and already sobered up and after emptying the keg, after cleaning up her parents' house, after putting people in their cars, we've brought the trash out to this dumpster by the beach and run out to put our bare feet in the sand. The water's quiet, moon reflected off the top and sharp and tinny, as the waves roll up; dark blues and blacks, as they dip down.

We each carried a large bag filled with empty cans and bottles, plastic cups, leftovers from the store-bought box cake we cooked too long and the big bowl of pasta that we mixed with garlic, oil, cheese, and diced tomatoes. We both smell of sweat and beer.

We've thrown a sort of week-late birthday party for her, while her mom and sister are traveling with her dad for work. No one except us knew it was a birthday party, and before the older kids arrived, from the larger public school ten miles from ours, we set out plates and napkins, knives and forks, and pretended we were grown. We poured glasses of wine and we dressed up and people looked confused when they came in and we told them to sit down, when later we brought the cake out and no one really knew what it was for.

We each did keg stands and our shirts rolled down our fronts, showing our bellies and our bras. I grabbed at my shirt, pushed back as it rolled down; she let hers sit around her neck. For a while, she went into her sister's room with some guy I run track with, about whom other girls at practice talk, to whom I've never said a word.

That wasn't fun, I say to Sasha now.

Which is maybe wrong, but also, she's the only person in the world to whom I say these things out loud.

They're all so dumb, she says.

She takes off her shirt and pants and I try not to stare.

Happy birthday, I say, thinking, *Why did we invite those people we don't like when we could have spent the whole night just like this.*

She laughs and nods down at my clothes.

You going in? she says.

It's January, but it's Florida, so it's warm, and I take off my shirt and pants.

We're both strong and swim out far and though the water shocks at first, it feels better, safer; I feel surer than I ever feel on land.

Back at her house, an hour later, we take hot showers and then wrap our hair up in towels and we sit on her big floral duvet and she talks and I half listen to the words she says, but also, I lie back and let her talk pour out overtop me until my eyes are closed. I don't sleep well most nights—I wander the high-ceilinged, too-still, too-big upstairs of my parents' house, talk online to older men, pretending that I'm someone else—but I sleep hours, ten or twelve, halfway through the next day, these nights that I'm with her.

2017

1

MY ALARM GOES off at 4:30 every weekday morning, and I keep my phone lodged between the slatted stairs that lead up to the lofted bed my husband built us in the closet we use as a bedroom, so that I'm not able to press Snooze. I climb down in the dark and find the phone, which has often fallen. I turn off the alarm and put on my bra and tights and shirt and shoes and gloves and headband, grab my keys and phone, and lock the door behind me; I run miles and miles before anyone wakes up.

By 6:15, I've showered and dressed and started to make breakfast. Sometimes my husband slips into the shower while the children are still asleep and we have sex. It's cold in the bathroom. He bends me over the railing of the back ledge. He pushes me up against the grimy tiles, holds my leg up. My body is outside the halo of hot water and my skin mottles and I shiver and am cold as I wait for him to come.

I take two trains to get to work and neither of them runs well. I wait sometimes three minutes for the first, sometimes fifteen. Sometimes, the train's right there, doors already open, as I pass through the turnstile, and I run, my bags flapping against my hip and back, up the stairs and through the crowd of people, slipping through the closing doors. I often get no seat and stand, trying not to grab hold of close-by arms or shoulders as the train turns hard, stops short. I try to read a book but fall asleep if I'm sitting and almost fall over if I stand. I hold it open, not turning any pages, both my bags clutched between by my calves and ankles, planting my feet firmly on the ground.

Good morning, team! says the Google chat they made me install on my phone when I started at this job six months ago. *Looking forward to a joyfully driven professional day!*

On Twitter, the world is ending. A nuclear war is threatening, ice caps are melting, kids at school are shooting other kids at school. At work, I wear collared shirts and cardigans and black wool dress pants and clip a set of keys around my neck and no one makes much mention of the world outside.

Once a week, more sometimes, when I get a seat on the train and am tired enough not to acknowledge what I'm doing, I check Sasha's mostly dormant Facebook—she has college photos and a handful from right after. A girl with whom she roomed her sophomore year, whom I knew vaguely, reposts the same handful of old photos every couple years; *We were so young!* this girl says, every time that it comes up, *look at us.* Twenty-year-old Sasha stares at me, over and over, too much how I remember: defiant, careless posture, perfect face, her too-big eyes.

I check her hardly active Twitter. Three years ago, she retweeted a *New Yorker* article on Miami Beach and climate change.

I check her sister's and her mother's Facebooks—sometimes she's in their pictures—to be sure that she's still there.

At work, two blocks north of the subway, in a big brick building, through two large, heavy doors, I walk past the scanners where the kids stand in line to have their bodies and their books checked. I tip my coffee to the security guards and the kids I know.

A handful of them call out my last name.

I take attendance on the live attendance tracker and talk to my two co–homeroom teachers, who are my only friends at work. They are black women, and I'm white; for a long time they didn't trust me, until one day they decided they could trust me, and still sometimes it seems like they might not. We are all older than our other colleagues; one of my two co–homeroom teachers is the only other person in this building with a kid. They didn't trust me because they shouldn't trust me, because there's so much I don't know or understand about them, because sometimes I lie to them about my upbringing to make my life seem more like theirs.

I think they trust me mostly because we love the kids we teach.

We check the various apps and Google calendars where the deliverables for the day are laid out and we post the morning PowerPoint about the new lateness policy, about the new rules concerning the dress code: only black socks are permitted, shirts must be tucked in at all times and belts worn, shoes must be black and sneakers aren't allowed.

I teach two classes in the morning, both Junior Literature and Language, and my job's completely fine as long as I am with my students. We read *Hamlet* and they raise their hands. I've been given a curriculum, rote and predictable, test-prep focused, but I ignore it. We read and we have conversations. They do group work, stand up together and give presentations on chart paper. My students are all black and brown kids, *underserved*, reduced- or free-lunch charter-school kids. They are still daily—by the shoddy, half-assed education that they're getting every day at this place, from grown-ups who mostly look like me—being underserved.

I catch a kid on his phone in my first class of the day and he smiles at me and looks five so I don't reprimand him. *Put it away*, I say, trying to look angry. There is a system that we're meant to use for discipline. Infractions: majors, minors. I have not installed this system on my phone. I have not, in the five months so far that I've been teaching at this institution—we spent one month before that training—given out one of these infractions.

My coteacher is twenty-four and does not know how to be a teacher. He also does not know how to interact with other humans or how to define the word "soliloquy." He stands in the back of the room and tries to give kids infractions and I tell him not to or take them away later, logging on to the system on my computer and disappearing the detentions he's doled out. He crosses his arms over his chest and tells kids to sit up or push their chairs in. Mr. D, they call him, instead of his full name, and he shakes his head. *That's not my name*, he says. And the kids laugh and, halfhearted, say they're sorry; a few minutes later, they call him Mr. D again.

Mr. D, they say, *I have to pee this minute*.

He clenches his fists.

But really, they say, *it's an emergency, Mr. D.*

Not now, he says.

I pop my head up from the student paper that I'm reading, trying to tell whoever said this without talking that they should stop it, but also, if they don't stop it, I will understand.

Go, I say, to the kid who still has to use the bathroom.

Mr. D stands quiet, his jaw tighter, eyes set on me, and no one speaks to him for the rest of class.

At lunch, my two co–homeroom teachers sit with me and we talk shit about our coworkers instead of reminding the kids to clean up after themselves and not swear, like we've been asked to do. We talk about the twenty-four-year-olds, my coteacher and the others: twenty-three, or twenty-six, but all the same. The young ones, almost all white, anxious, energetic; their sentences sound like questions at the end. They seem scared of their own students; they don't know how to teach and no one's tried to help them. They're held to standards they can't meet—based on test scores and class averages—and they panic and dole out the material in the exact rote way that we're meant not to. If and when their methods do not work, they blame the kids.

They're not awful, these young white teachers. I talk about them because I'm manipulative and unfair, because I've learned the best way to bond with colleagues is to be galvanized against other colleagues, against bosses, and I'm desperate to ally myself with my two co–homeroom teachers instead. These twenty-four-year-olds: I've sat with some of them, in one of the classrooms we use as an office when no one's using it for teaching; they're so young, and if they were my students, they'd be some of my favorites. We've had coffee, sat together during training. They're sweet and talk earnestly about social justice, but they're my colleagues, not my students, and they can't see and don't seem to want to see all the ways their good intentions aren't worth much.

Some days, I move to the tables with the kids from my class, kids I caught sleeping or who didn't turn in their homework. *You want to eat lunch with me,* I say. And they shake their heads but smile. They tell jokes mostly, making fun of one another. *Miz,* they say, and then they say my last name, *you know Jalen has a crush on Aminata; you know Razaq didn't even read that shit you thought he talked about so well last class; you know Ananda posted a Snap about Nashya's man and now they ain't talking and Nashya's going to go find her after school.*

Man, huh? I say, and they laugh at me.

You got a man, Miz, they say, and I nod, smiling at them, and they laugh again.

After lunch there is a break and I download and print out all my pay stubs because I need them to finish filing for bankruptcy.

How's it going? asks one of the math teachers as I use the printer in the teacher workroom. The math teacher is also twenty-four and wears a tie, a dark-blue jacket, and a crisp white shirt with the collar buttoned every day. He has bright-white teeth and perfect posture, too much facial hair. I check to make sure I have all of my pay stubs as he looks over my shoulder, and I turn my body so I know he knows I don't want him to look.

Joyfully driven, I say.

We share the building with five other schools and the track team has nowhere to practice so they practice in the hallways during the last four periods of the day. I leave the teacher workroom and wait, pressed against the hall wall, as kids fly by over hurdles. A girl's toe catches on the bottom of a hurdle and it bangs against the hard, dark floor and she falls, hands flat on the cold tile, and she doesn't scream. I check in my bag for my pay stubs over and over. I check Twitter, check and recheck email, half read student work, and input grades. I'm not as good a teacher as I wish I were. I'm inconsistent, get distracted. I give fifty-seven comments on every three-page paper, and the next day I skim through to make sure everybody turned in their work, fix a few grammar or comprehension errors, and give almost everyone a B. No one reads my comments, and the work feels most productive when I'm one-on-one with students, checking in before and after class and making time for conferences. Most of the writing is difficult to track and the reading of it, hour after hour, wears on my brain.

Our older daughter's school calls three hours before the workday's over. They never remember that they're supposed to call my husband, who is home during the week and takes care of them while I'm at work. Our daughter got a bead stuck in her nose. I must come pick her up and take her to a doctor who can get it out. I almost tell the nurse to call my husband, then instead I say I'll be right there and message my boss that I have to leave. My co–homeroom teacher and I are the only people on the staff with kids and usually, when I say "kids" to any of my other coworkers, people's eyes glaze over and they get antsy and uncomfortable and I get out of things.

I'm not yet on the subway platform when our daughter's school calls back to say they got the bead out. The other nurse, who had been on her lunch break, held her hand over our daughter's face, her thumb pressed hard against her unobstructed nostril, and blew into our daughter's mouth until the bead popped out.

So we don't need you, says the woman. *She's back in class,* she says, *all good.*

But I'm already out, and my coat's on and I keep walking. I skip the subway. When I was very young and single, without children, I used to walk the city for days. I head north then west and walk into the Guggenheim. There is a retrospective of stark lines and colors. I can't remember the last time I've been in a museum on a weekday, and I walk very slowly up the corkscrewing path and am alone and quiet. I look a long time at each painting. It feels like what I imagine people feel like when they imagine whatever god they might believe in standing close to them.

I walk from the museum to the train and take it downtown, where I get off and go to a coffee shop I used to go to before I worked full time. I was in grad school for six years—English literature, mid- to late twentieth century, British and American, forgotten or actively discarded female writers: Penelope Fitzgerald, Anita Brookner, Jean Rhys, Nella Larsen, Lucia Berlin. There was a time when I thought giving books to other people—showing them their richness, their quiet, secret, temporary safety—could be a useful way to spend one's life. I spent another five years as a part-time adjunct, waitress, admin assistant. Once, for six months, I wrote quizzes to accompany the bad books put out by an education corporation, but I was fired because I couldn't keep my sentences short enough.

This—the school, at thirty-four—is the first full-time job of my whole life.

I used to come here almost every day while I wrote my dissertation and to grade papers after. Even a year ago, I came once or twice a week. I know the name of the girl behind the counter because it's the same as my name, different spelling, and we used to joke about this when she asked my name so she could call it when my coffee was ready. But this time when she asks my name and I tell her and I start to smile, thinking she remembers, she just nods and inputs it into the computer and counts out my change.

I tip her, too much, still smiling, hoping she'll remember. I find a window seat. I have the same book I never read on the train and I open it and read it: Patrick Modiano, *Paris Nocturne*. It's strange and magic; there's a car crash and then almost nothing happens. I sip my coffee and break off tiny pieces of the cookie that I've ordered. My husband texts me, *How's your day?*

Okay, I say.

An hour after work ends I pack up my bag. There's a new group of people on either side of me since I started reading. My coffee's empty. The cookie's gone.

Honey, I hear, as I get in the elevator.

I turn to see our neighbor. *Josslyn*, I say. She's my favorite person in the building. She stands close to me and holds my elbow as she asks me questions. She's in her sixties, could pass for forty. She wears large wool cardigans in bright colors and keeps her tight-curled hair cut close. She has large eyes and I look forward, always, to the next time her rough, warm hands grab hold of me.

How are you? she says.

Shitty, I say.

It is our game, has been for the six years we've lived here, to never answer one another's how are yous with *fine, good, okay, you know*.

She laughs at me. *Me too*, she says, as we get off the elevator.
Kiss the girls, she says, as she lets herself into her apartment.
I will, I say, letting myself into mine.

How was your day? my husband asks as I walk through the door and take off my shoes and he makes dinner. The whole place smells of onions, garlic, a poblano pepper. I hug the children, hold them, kiss them, give them extra from Josslyn. The two-year-old crawls onto my lap to nurse.

Fine, I say.

We give them a bath and eat and put them to bed and watch TV—seldom anything so engaging that we can't also both do two or three things on our phones or our computers. We climb up to bed.

I read Jean Rhys, *Good Morning, Midnight*. *I would feel as if I were drugged, sitting there, watching those damned dolls*, says the main character, of the porcelain dolls at a shop where she once worked, *thinking what a success they would have made of their lives if they had been women.*

My husband falls asleep.

At 4:45 I run along the water and it's freezing and it starts to rain but I keep running. Rats sit out in the open, on top of benches, on the concrete. One runs overtop my foot and I scream and jump and no one sees.

On the subway, I see a new picture of Sasha's sister: she got a dog with her newly live-in boyfriend and there is some pithy caption about this being baby number one.

I teach my morning class and at the after-lunch staff meeting our principal, who is thirty-one, posts a large yellow box on the smartboard with the number twenty-five inside. Twenty-five of us missed the weekend deliverable of inserting our lesson plans into the task grid established by the CEO the week before. The email we got from our principal as a result of this missed deliverable was long and scolding, bullet pointed. It was written in the tone one might reserve for a small child. All but one of us, our principal tells us, have since turned in the task grid. He posts a second square, this one red, with the number nineteen. *And this*, he says, his small eyes sharpening, *is the number of you who did not reply to my email alerting you to this missed weekend deliverable with contrition and gratitude*.

After the meeting, I go into the classroom where I keep my coat and bag and get them. I've already taught my classes. I'm meant to be somewhere, planning, but we have no set office. I go down the escalator and no one sees me leaving. I think if they see me I'll say I'm going for a late lunch, have to get the children. Now that I'm out here, I have no idea why I've stayed in the building all this time.

The subway's much less crowded in the middle of the day. I have a seat plus room to set both my bags beside me. I read Gayl Jones, *Corregidora*: generations carrying and passing violences to one another, how hard it is to learn what we don't know to learn, the specific ways that we might try to cast ourselves anew.

On the bench across from me a woman has laid down a large plastic bag and is asleep.

I get a coffee and a cookie at the coffee shop and read my book for all the other hours that I'm meant to be at work and then I go home on the train.

How was your day? says my husband when I get home as he makes dinner. I hug and kiss our children, nurse the baby.

I bathe them and we eat together. *Family read?* asks the two-year-old when I go to read them books, put them to sleep. I call my husband and we all lie on the baby's bed together. I read and she sits on me. The four-year-old sits on her dad's lap and it's warmer in here than any other place in our apartment, and halfway through the second book I fall asleep. An hour later, I'm still in there, and my husband comes to get me. He helps me free my arm from the two-year-old's small hands and stands behind me as I climb the ladder up to bed and follows up right after; he wraps his arm around my waist.

At 4:50 the next morning I pass a man, fully dressed in a too-thin coat, while I run underneath the highway. He smells, up close, like liquor, and as I run by, he screams a high-pitched scream and I sprint until I've covered another mile and know for sure he's far away.

Sasha's liked her little sister's Facebook picture of her dog.

I teach a night class uptown on Thursdays—I keep the night class even though I mostly know by now I'll never get a real job from the institution where I teach this night class; I mostly know that real jobs at institutions like this don't exist anymore. I keep the job because I spent all those years in school and mostly I've forgotten what I thought they might be worth. Because it feels good sometimes, pretending, that I got what I set out to get.

I often stay late at work these days to meet with students, help with papers, but my coteacher comes to say he wants to meet with me to talk about *relational concerns*, and I say I can't because my kids' school just called and then I leave and go to a dark bar uptown and sip a raspberry-flavored gin drink and read my book before I have to teach.

In my night class, we read Imre Kertész, *Kaddish for an Unborn Child*. A student who sits off to the side of the table we all sit at, though there's still room, and who has strangely dyed red hair, raises her hand and says, *The main character is mansplaining Auschwitz to his wife*, and I say, *But she wasn't there and is actively refusing to try to understand*, and she says, *Typical*, and we move on.

On Thursdays the children go to sleep without me and it's late and the subway's mostly empty for the hour that I ride it. *We filed*, my husband says about the bankruptcy, and I'm still drunk, or maybe I'm hungover, from the drink before I taught and I do not want to talk so I kiss him and reach my hand underneath his shirt and we have sex on our loft bed. I hit my head and he says, *Sorry*, and then he comes and falls asleep and I stay up and read.

When we met I was in graduate school and he was still, for that first year, a person who wore suits. I had a small apartment uptown and he'd sneak out of work and I'd get out of class and we would fuck standing up against the hall wall by the entrance, me sometimes up on the kitchen counter, hands grasping the cheap vinyl. I would come and he would too and we'd both pull our pants back up and he'd go back to work and I'd go to the comp class I taught in the afternoon still smelling of him.

He'd last a full year at that job before he left to do custom carpentry for the sorts of people that he used to work with, hoping it'd be more one day, a store of handmade furniture from reclaimed wood. I was so proud then. We were eighties babies, born of plenty, cloistered by our whiteness and the places we were raised in—his parents didn't have much money, neither had a college education, but we were both brought up to think that if we checked off certain boxes we'd be fine.

9/11 happened my second week of college; the financial crisis came the year after we met. It would be years before we understood the implications of these chasms; we weren't formed enough to see them, were too safe to feel their first round of hits. We made so many choices based on what we thought the world was, what it wasn't any longer, what we'd been told it was but what we finally understand that it had never been.

He worked for Lehman Brothers when the markets crashed and they went under—the sky was falling everywhere, except, of course, that he could just have found another job like that. He had this idea, we both did, that he did not want to be implicated any longer in the abstract mess of numbers on a screen and people's lives all made or broken. We had principles or something, made up almost wholly out of things we knew we didn't want to be or have a part in more than any concrete plans for what we'd be instead. I vaguely thought books were the answer, because they'd saved me and that seemed like something: to give them to other people, to expose them to them. He thought working with his hands. We were galvanized in this way, smug and stupid. It felt athletic and exciting, this misguided, blind self-righteousness.

Now, I think mostly he still likes what he does, except, of course, when work is slow or bills are due.

It's 5:20 and I'm running late. I've stayed up late rereading Marguerite Duras, *The Lover*: *Very early in my life it was too late*. A man in his sixties gives himself a quiet, thoughtful pep talk as he climbs the steepest hill on the south side of the park at a jog as I sprint by.

You're not doing enough "I" speak, says my supervisor as we sit with the twenty-four-year-old to talk about his relational concerns. He says I am condescending to him. Which is not wrong. I tried to talk to him about the fact that the kids hate him without telling him that the kids hate him, and now I hate him too.

I try to explain this. I try to say as carefully, as diplomatically, as I can that I have absolutely said the wrong things in trying to talk to him, that I should have never put him on the spot and asked him his age in front of other colleagues, but that the kids are turning on him, he treats them like they're preschoolers, and that's not good for anyone.

You need to focus on how you're responsible, what you've *done in each of these situations,* says my supervisor. She is twenty-seven. *I hear you talking too much about what* he *has done.*

She calls us both by our names often, because it was in a book she read about how to interact with people and mediate conflict between colleagues. I know this because she has it with her and it's covered in yellow and pink Post-its.

I teach another class and then I get my bag and coat and walk downtown until I hit a CVS, where I buy a large box of the sour neon gummy worms that I stopped eating when I was pregnant the first time and afraid of anything that might be processed or chemically enhanced getting through to the baby, and then I kept not eating them because I was nursing, and then pregnant again, and then never outside the house without our children when I was not at work. I'm still nursing, but I buy them and open the bag on the sidewalk as I walk to a movie theater I remember from when I used to be a waitress seven blocks away. There are so many streets like this, where I have been so many different people. If anyone were to ask me why I can't leave even as this city is too hard for not-rich people, I would say it's because I'm too afraid of what would happen to all these different people somewhere else. This is the place where I was formed, long after forming should have happened; it's the place where no one was looking and I felt allowed.

It's what I imagine home would feel like if the home that I was born into had felt safe.

We have one credit card that somehow inexplicably still works, though all the others have been canceled, and I buy a ticket to a movie on it and I sit and watch a story about other people's lives in the dark in the middle of the day.

On my train ride home, I get an email from a former student at the university where I teach my night class. She's twenty-something, young and anxious. I remember she wore crop tops in winter and wide-legged pants; she had long blond hair. In class, she used to work her hair into tiny braids, then chew on them, letting them fall out of her mouth wet when she raised her hand to speak. She spooned one large tub of yogurt into her mouth with a white plastic spoon in the first hour of every class, and the bright white skin of her bare arms and shoulders would splotch red when she talked.

hey! says her email, no capital letters and hardly any punctuation. *wondering if i could pop by your office hours sometime next week*. The way she piles phrase on top of phrase without saying why she wants to meet makes me worry for her.

I'm up there Thursdays, I type, though I'm an adjunct and do not have an office. *Let's find a time,* I say.

It's Sasha's birthday, I say to my husband on the weekend. We have one day a week together, since he works on Sundays, and we pack snacks and a change of underwear for both the children and we go into the city, to the Whitney, also on the magic credit card. The kids make paintings that look like the paintings that are hanging and then we walk around until the two-year-old starts crying on the floor because we won't let her touch the painted birds even though they are her favorite color, purple, and we go home.

You should call her, says my husband.

He used to make a face every time I said her name. But now he starts to cook dinner, gets a beer out of the refrigerator, tells the children they have to clean up their Legos before they can use the iPad, makes me a second drink.

Why not? he says now.

I guess, I say.

Did she call you on your birthday? he says.

Mommy, says our four-year-old, *who's Sasha?*

I text her and she says thanks right away and sends me an emoji.

I hate emojis. As if, all of a sudden, we have agreed that words don't work.

Sorry I missed yours, she says.

I wait a week. On the day that I watch the kids alone and my husband works, I let them watch TV in the back room, even though we try mostly not to let them watch TV, and they eat granola bars and chips for lunch. I only vaguely, in the background, imagine my husband asking what protein they've had so far today. I read my book most of the morning: *The Time of the Doves,* Mercè Rodoreda—the Spanish Civil War and a young and battered housewife; her husband forces her to care for the doves he keeps; he beats her, refuses to call her by her name; he leaves to fight in the war and she and the children nearly starve until the kind grocer asks her to marry him, feeds them, saves the day.

We spend the afternoon together on the front stoop with Josslyn. They chalk the sidewalk and she brings out coffee, touching me three times, the elbow twice and then the shoulder, and she yells at the twenty-something boy who lets his dog pee in the planter that she's set out front.

How were they? my husband asks when he gets home and I've managed to give them food and get them bathed and read to them until they fell asleep.

Great, I say.

He kisses me and we order Thai food on the magic credit card—I sit on the phone as the man on the other end goes to run it. I wait for him to tell me that it doesn't work, but he comes back twenty seconds later; *Twenty minutes,* he says, although it always takes over an hour.

Congrats on the wedding, I text Sasha, after we've gone to bed and I'm reading again but also scrolling through Twitter. *Sad we missed it,* I say. Which is as aggressive as I can be, which is still couched in the passive, which is usually more artful, but it's a text message, and also, I'm not sure I care if my aggression is not pacified.

I spend an hour as my husband sleeps, rescrolling through the Facebook pictures of her California destination wedding. I reclick through the profiles of the four women who stood next to her as she smiled in her lace strapless dress and held the hand of a tall, dashing man. One of these women is her sister, who landed just shy of Sasha and her mother's perfect features. She holds her shoulders back, though, and grins straight at the camera, willing it, it seems, to find her just right as she is.

I WAS THIRTEEN and she was fourteen and we were high school freshmen. A boy I thought I loved loved her, and I stayed on the phone with him sometimes late at night discussing her. I think I thought that if I listened hard or well or long enough that he'd love me instead. Instead, they broke up, and he stopped calling. And then there she was. I knew everything about her that any breathing person would love, the way she felt and talked as if she were a grown-up; the way she was smart but also pretty but also didn't care enough about being cool to use the power that she should have had to have more friends. Whether I wanted to love or have or just to be her never felt as easily discernible as this or that, one or the other—more like all of it, and then more, at once.

We had a class together and our teacher was sick for half the year and the sub sat at the desk reading a book and we sat in the back of the room and *talked*. "Talked" does not begin to hold inside it what we did together. We sat in the school-issue chairs attached to desks, my knees up to my chest. She wore her hair down, curly, with product in it that made her smell grown-up. I don't remember the words we said but that sometimes they felt so alive they had to be whispered; we had to lean close to each other, bottoms of our desk-chairs screeching. Sometimes one of us got so loud that other kids, or whatever sub we had that week, would turn from their desks and look.

You know, says Sasha, looking at me. I'm fourteen and she's fifteen. She goes to touch me, then thinks better of it. We're always close but don't often embrace. Her family is a touching, hugging unit; when people reach for me, I never know what to do with all my limbs. *You might*—she's scrutinizing. I know I'm turning red. She reaches down and touches my ponytail. *You might be prettier*—she wouldn't say just "pretty." It's important she gives me that, no matter what. It's a word she's always had a right to, a world she will always, easily, possess. *I mean, you're pretty, naturally*. She smiles. I can't stand this kind of looking. *But if we let your hair down*—she takes out the rubber band. My hair is nearly black and thick, and though I always wear it up, when loose, it reaches to the middle of my back. I feel my spine rounding, my shoulders closing in. *Do a little something, not too much, but something to accentuate your eyes.*

She teaches me things mothers are supposed to teach: how to use a tampon, apply mascara, find a bra that fits. How to talk out loud about ideas I've only let form in my head.

Sometimes, after school, we go to her house and hang out with her mom. Her family has less money than my family. The concept of money is sufficiently safe for me at this age, available without acting as a hindrance, that both its presence and its lack feel equally abstract. My mother's ostentatious car, vacations twice a year, our massive house; the too-big boxes of cereal and jars of peanut butter stored in Sasha's pantry from the Costco half an hour away, their biggish house passed down and things breaking all the time and nothing getting fixed. My mom works sixty-hour weeks and when we sit down for dinner at nine or ten—because that's when she's gotten home, but also, she wants to make my sister and me dinner—she and my father ask us the grades we got on tests, my times on the track. There is always too much food, so much food, made with cheese and milk and butter and my sister and I learn slowly—because we've been taught since we were very small that fat is lazy and disgusting—that we have to either only pretend that we are eating or eat only this meal every day. We sit across from each other, our mother and our father at either end of the table. They spend the time leading up to dinner talking about work. My mom cooks and my dad makes the drinks, one and a half shots of gin with tonic for my mother, a whiskey and Diet Coke for my dad. They have these before dinner and then wine and beer with dinner, one and then another. My sister and I linger in our rooms or on the outskirts of the kitchen. We do homework, watch TV. Both our parents change out of their suits. When we sit down, the TV's on, but we talk over it for the first twenty minutes. *How was practice?* asks my father. My sister doesn't run and hates this part. *Fine,* I say, most of the time. *We did speed today,* I say. It's understood I won if we did a speed workout. Sometimes I tell the stories that I know most please them: that I lapped some of the slower girls during intervals, that Coach sent me to run with the boys again. I hate running with the boys and do not talk the whole time and they seem to hate me even more when we have finished. They all need to stay at least a step ahead of me and we run faster than we're supposed to. None of us is willing to let the other beat them, and it's hot and humid and we come back sweating, panting; none of them look at me the whole time. We come back angry, our legs and arms and shoulders tight; we suck down water, and the girls are already back and waiting, hardly sweating, and they all talk together and I pour water over my head and walk back to my car or ride alone. *How was math?* my dad asks, because I'm in an advanced math class, was skipped ahead at their request, and this is something that he likes to ask about. *Fine,* I say again. I'm not as good at it as they think and I lose focus. I feel too young; everyone else feels so much older, and I sit in back and read a book in my lap as the teacher talks. My sister is a champion debater and I'm grateful when the focus turns to her and what she's done or won or how she is preparing for her next competition. Her grades are not as good as my grades. She's in fewer advanced classes, tests less well than I do, and my father often looks less interested when it's her turn to speak. She eats lunch, I know, alone in the debate room. She's two years younger than me and I drive her to school once I turn sixteen and get a car, but we seldom talk.

Sasha's mom bakes and asks us about boys. She is a guidance counselor at the elementary school and very smart. When Sasha's sister's home she sits with us also and often interrupts. They all touch each other. Her sister fixes Sasha's hair or asks midsentence if she can borrow the earrings that she's wearing, where she got that sweater, if she thinks the shirt that she's wearing suits her frame. She gestures often and I flinch when I sit close to her. Their mom looks hard at whichever of us is speaking and when Sasha and her sister fight in their brash, sharp way of fighting, she says, *Girls*, in this specific, intimate way that both makes them look at each other like she's being silly, talking to them like they're children, and also makes them stop, look up at her, say *sorry* quietly.

Of her and her sister, Sasha's the more aberrant. She fights more often with their mother. She is the smarter of the two but also the more reckless, the one who needs more guidance, more taking care. Her sister often scolds her in my presence. I think part of what Sasha likes about me is how rootless I am, feral maybe, that she's the one in charge.

Even though my parents are never home, we always go to her house. My house is so clean it makes the few other kids I've had over uncomfortable. It's big and cavernous, with lots of suede and dark wood. My room is upstairs, down a long hall, my sister's room down an opposite hall on the other side, and my parents sometimes, if they come home from work and we're in our rooms, have to call the upstairs phone line to see if we are there.

When I turn sixteen I get a brand-new black convertible, just exactly what I asked for—I don't know until years later to be embarrassed by it—and Sasha and I drive out by the water on the weekends, top down, sun splotched on our faces, hair a mess. I skip school by myself; her mom has friends who work at the high school and they would tell her. When the school calls to say I wasn't there, I just delete the message before anybody sees. I drive out to the beach and run, then walk, for hours and no one notices at dinner that there's sand still on my feet and in my hair. I drive around and cry. My face is swollen in addition to being sunburned and I look straight at my mother as she asks me about my calc grade and she nods when I tell her it's an A.

Our senior year, Sasha has a boyfriend much older than us all. He is at the community college and in plays. I think he's awful and then worry I'm just jealous: of him or her, I'm not quite sure. He's dramatic, gesturing and talking, saying nothing, but she says she loves him. We talk about him on the phone for hours. He gets us stoned on weekends at the beach and convinces us to break in to old hotel pools at night and sit naked in the hot tub, four or five girls and his one or two friends that always tag along—they don't ever touch me—and he tells us stories about places he says he's been. We play Truth or Dare and we are told to kiss. She grabs the back of my head and burrows her lips in my face and I breathe through my nose and my hands make small, tight fists.

It's five degrees so I wear two pairs of tights and two shirts and a jacket that my mother bought me for Christmas that smells because I wear it almost every day. I wear a headband and gloves. There's a hole in the index finger of my right glove and though every other part of me is covered up and warm my finger is raw and splotched and I have no feeling in my hand when I get home.

My husband slips in the shower as I stand underneath the spray, cold skin prickling with each drop of heat, my legs and arms bright red. I make a fist and then unfist it over and over, trying to get the feeling back. My husband pulls back the curtain and I have to step out from underneath the warmth to let him in. I put my hand along his back and he gasps and snaps at me and we both shampoo and condition and scrub our arms and legs and faces without speaking, without touching, until we're out and dry and dressed.

At work, a woman whom I've always liked but don't really speak to is putting on lipstick in the employee bathroom. *How are you?* I say, and her eyes angle toward her lipstick and she says, *I'm hoping this will pick me up*.

Will you teach me? I say, unable, it seems, just to smile. I blame my mother, I think, for my inability to not always try in some way to make conversation out of quiet. I point to her bag. *Those bags remain one of the great mysteries of my life*, I say.

She laughs.

You don't need it, she says. She is younger than me, just like every other person who works here, and she is also trying to be nice.

I smile at her and shake my head. *My poor daughters,* I say.

I leave after the last class I teach with the twenty-four-year-old, in which he gives a fifteen-minute speech about Brita filters as a metaphor for making edits on one's papers. *Clarity,* he says, *and purity*. The kids' eyes glaze over and I catch a girl in the back playing pool on her phone but I pretend that I don't see her and as soon as class is over I grab my bag and coat and take the escalator steps two at a time.

I keep checking my phone as I walk down Broadway, thinking Sasha might call or text me back. I don't want her to call me. I use the magic credit card to get more gummy candy from the CVS and one of those tubes of goop meant to put underneath one's eyes and walk over the Brooklyn Bridge—though I usually reserve the bridge for running—and the last three miles to our apartment as it gets dark and my ears are very cold.

2

IT SNOWED, THEN rained, and now ice has frozen on the sidewalks. I sit up in bed, scrolling through my phone and thinking myself through the pros and cons of going running. I won't be able to breathe at work if I don't go running. If I fall and break something, I won't be able to breathe for months. I put on two pairs of tights and two shirts—one fleece and one thin insulate, both long-sleeved—and the padded jacket my mom got me that still smells. I put the band around my head and I put on my gloves, still with the single hole, and I pull a fleece tube around my neck so I can yank it up to just below my eyes in the moment when I start to lose feeling in my nose and lips. I run in the middle of the road so I won't slip, as the sidewalks are still slick with ice and piles of snow, and cars drive slowly past the few times they drive past. I see one other person running, a woman, older than me, slowly climbing through the snow piled on the sidewalk, taking off.

At lunch, at work, my co–homeroom teacher shows me a YouTube video of a black woman prepping a wig and placing it, firmly, on her head. She cuts the hair and shapes it as it sits on a mannequin in front of her. She colors the scalp to match her skin tone with what looks like chalk but my co–homeroom teacher says is not. Her hair is held against her head in small tight braids and she slips the wig overtop and shifts it back, then right, then left until it sits perfectly on her head.

You do that every day? I say, setting down her phone, as she eats the mozzarella sticks that come with French fries that they serve on Tuesdays, neither of which I can quite bring myself to eat.

My friend laughs at me. I stay mostly quiet because I do not want her to stop telling me things like she did this morning: out of nowhere, holding my arm and whispering to me, as the kids filed into the classroom and we sipped our third cups of coffee, *You know my hair's a wig.*

I did not, I said.

Now she shows me this clip and then another, a different woman, a different type of wig. She explains to me the names and types of textures: 4A, 4B, 4C. She shows me another video of different types of braids.

My hair is short and, while we watch the video, I keep reaching up to touch it, embarrassed, maybe, by the ease of it. How I only ran my fingers through it, still wet from my shower after my run, as I left the house this day.

Kids walk past us and my co–homeroom teacher whispers to me. *Her hair is natural,* she says, nodding toward one girl and then another, *her hair's a weave, a wig; worst of all,* she tells me, her face close to mine and her whisper getting quieter, nodding toward a girl carrying a tray of double mozzarella sticks, *this girl, against any thinking person's working knowledge of the fact that this is basically giving in to white supremacy, has somehow been allowed to get her hair relaxed.*

My co–homeroom teachers, more and more, share things like this with me, but also, they have a text chain with the three other black teachers at school, of which I am not—I know better than to ever ask to be—a part. I'm quiet more than I'm used to. I let them talk and try very hard to stay still and to listen and, every time they tell me things, I feel like I've lived a whole life without knowing anything and I'm so grateful that they trust me at least enough for this.

I keep separate from them also. They don't know about my leaving. They don't know about my night class. They don't know that we pay extra rent to live in a neighborhood we can't afford so that our kids can go to a school that's said to be better than the one my co–homeroom teacher's kid will go to when he turns four next year.

I stay through the end of the day and help students with the paper I've assigned, which all of them are not quite comprehending. I've asked them to use one character in *Hamlet* to explore the gradations either of sanity or of culpability throughout. They're too set on the desire to state one thing or the other—Ophelia's *absolutely* insane, they want to argue; Hamlet's *absolutely* just defending his father's honor, they tell me. *But what about*, I say, pointing to a different moment, and they keep getting tripped up. They've never written anything longer than two pages, never been taught to cite sources. Their syntax twists and slips in this strange performance of an idea of academic prose that has been delivered to them by their teachers before. It obfuscates whatever it is they might be trying to say, and I sit with them and ask, one by one, *But what do you want to say?* and they tell me, and I say, *So why don't you write that?*

I can't parse what of this is them being kids and what is having not been taught. In grad school, I taught comp, and there was plenty that my students couldn't think or do. But there is something fundamental at this school that I can't make sense of. What's taken for granted about these kids is different than what was taken for granted about us when I was at my cloistered, white, and wealthy public school. Too many of the teachers, nearly all of the administrators, think our kids can't think or do things that at my school we were told we had no choice but to think and do. Discipline stands in the place of any opportunity for exploration. Teachers try sometimes to teach the way we're told they want us to be teaching, *progressive, emphasizing inquiry and exploration*, but then no one seems to trust the kids can learn if information isn't delivered to them in small, concisely bullet-pointed worksheets and PowerPoints, so teachers summarize and truncate the information, covering themselves, too afraid of all the ways our performances are judged wholly on the scores kids get on tests.

The kids have learned to expect that this is the only way to learn. When I ask questions but don't give answers in advance, I see not only how scared they are, because no one here has taught them how to trust their ability to think, I see how desperate for it they are, how exciting and surprising and specific their brains are.

When we sit together after school I keep a store of Doritos and Kit Kats and Reese's cups from the teacher workroom on my desk, and as their theses start to clear up and their sentences begin to build more seamlessly together, we take breaks to eat and they make fun of my cardigans and my dress pants; they look at me long, head tilting toward one side, eyebrows cocked, and ask if I've ever thought of growing out my hair.

I skip my run the next morning because my back and legs and neck are sore, and I try to do a yoga video in the small room off our kitchen but I get bored. The woman talks as if I am her child and she just wants me to feel better. I mute her and lie back on the mat with my eyes closed until the children both wake up and come out and crawl overtop of me and the two-year-old reaches her hand up my shirt and asks to nurse.

I'm at a work meeting. We are discussing whether the new policy barring head wraps is professional or racist and what type of orthopedic shoes should be allowed with doctor's notes. The few times I've spoken up in meetings like this I've later been asked quietly by my boss not to any longer, so I sit in back and read the news on my phone.

I text with a friend from college, Leah, who is finally pregnant after three rounds of IVF and has just found out she's having twins.

I get an email that says a Chilean writer, name linked to her Wikipedia page in parentheses, would like to sit in on my Thursday night class at the university. The Chilean writer read your syllabus and responded intensely to it, says the email. I'm sitting in the back with my two co–homeroom teachers and they both look at me as our boss talks. I send the Chilean writer the title and the author of the book we're reading, as I'm requested to do, and turn my phone back over on my desk.

I teach one more class after our meeting and we have a debate about whether the ghost in *Hamlet* is real. I offer lunch on me as extra incentive for whoever wins. I give them ten minutes to plan their opening arguments. After that they craft rebuttals. After rebuttals come the cross-examinations and I egg both sides on, pointing out the holes in their opponents' theses, pointing out how their opponents' examples might be twisted to serve their arguments as well. We all get loud.

The twenty-four-year-old stands quietly in back. I think

maybe he's transcribing in his head the case he'll make when he goes to our boss to get me fired. I think if I get fired I won't mind. And then one of my students stands close to me, pointing to a moment in the text she thinks will help her team, and I think I will go over to the twenty-four-year-old and threaten to harm him bodily if he takes this job from me.

While the kids prep their closing arguments, I check my email. *I'm so honored*, the Chilean writer writes back to me, *I can't wait*.

Third-floor hall duty. I'm reading: Nawal El Saadawi, *Woman at Point Zero*. *All my life I have been searching for something that would fill me with pride, make me feel superior to everyone else, including kings, princes, and rulers*, says Firdaus, as she sits in a cell, sentenced to death.

I get a message about a girl, a tenth grader, who walks out of class because of anxiety. She has a disorder, we were told at a staff meeting—amplified flight reflex. If she feels anxious, she walks out of class, sometimes out of school, and she walks often. Regularly, on the Google chat, we get messages saying that she's gone.

Can someone check the third-floor bathroom? says the chat.

Got it, I message back.

Kayla? I say, looking under the stall doors.

Another student, who is in my class and is standing at the mirror, motions to me. *Last stall*, she mouths.

I knock and Kayla opens the stall door slowly. *I don't know you*, she says.

I don't teach the tenth graders. I introduce myself, tell her what I teach.

I still have to pee, she says, closing the door.

I message the Google chat. Minutes pass and no sound

comes from the stall. I watch the toes of her black lace-up shoes turn in.

She comes out and the toilet hasn't flushed. She turns the water on and washes and rewashes and rewashes her hands.

Come on, Kayla, I say. *We have to get you back to class.*

She doesn't look at me. She washes one more time and grabs a paper towel, placing it in between her fingers, folding it into a tiny dark-brown square before placing it into the trash.

We come out of the bathroom and I'm not sure if I'm allowed to touch her. I'm not sure how to make sure she doesn't run away without my touching her. I try to keep my voice calm and not to scold her. I have to chat the counselor to find out where to take her and I type with one finger, keeping one hand free in case she runs. She's taller than me but she stays half a step behind. Twice, she tries to turn back toward the bathroom and I grab hold of her backpack and half nudge, half lead her up the stairs.

What's your favorite subject? I say, suddenly dumb and bad at conversation.

Science, she says.

Cool, I say. *I like science.*

She tries to take a sharp left when we get up the stairs and I turn right and once again I have to grab her backpack to keep her with me. She's wily and she's fast, they told us in the meeting. I loop my arm around hers.

Come back, Kayla, I say as I let go of her to knock on the counselor's office door and she disappears down the hall.

She was just here, I say when the counselor comes out and Kayla's gone.

I leave after my hall duty is over. I pass the twenty-four-year-old on the escalator. He goes up and I go down and I look him in the eye and do not smile and he finally looks away.

The shift in register between my day job and my night job usually takes half an hour. The students that I teach at night are grad students. They're so much older, paying to be there. It is both more intellectually rigorous and not as hard for me because I don't have to convince them they should care. Because their lives up until now have all been more like mine. I'm less careful with them maybe; their out-of-class demands feel both less important to me and easier to solve.

I sit in whatever office I am given and I disappear for an hour, as long as students haven't asked to meet with me, and I read the book I'm meant to teach or I scroll through Twitter or text my husband and ask him to send me videos of our girls. I take off my blazer if I've been wearing a blazer. I have, twice this year, bought a T-shirt on the magic credit card after I looked in the mirror on my way uptown and felt too professionally dressed to teach literature to graduate students.

The Chilean writer is in her fifties, I learned from the link embedded in the earlier email form the school administration office, and has written five novels, three of them translated into English. She is on her second marriage, has one grown son. She sits next to me at the seminar table as we discuss Clarice Lispector's *The Passion According to* G. H., a novel that has attempted to absence words of their meaning. *Before I entered the room, what was I?* G. H. asks. Most of the students did not like it. I have told them that like and dislike are not pertinent but they are incapable of not telling everybody whether or not they liked each book we read. *It's a hard novel and it doesn't give much space for the reader to feel grounded, to get inside it,* I say. *Why does it do this, though?* I ask. I gesture too much when I teach. In the novel, a woman stands at the edge of a room and watches the slow death of the cockroach she's decapitated with a door, talking with it, before ingesting its entrails.

A female student who wears dark eyeliner and has long curly hair raises her hand close to the end of class and says, of the experience of reading the novel, *I felt hit by a truck*. Some students laugh, and I say, *So, then, she made you feel something. So, then,* I say, *did she succeed in that?*

The Chilean writer stays quiet the whole time. She takes notes. She smiles and nods whenever I look toward her and when the student says the thing about the truck she laughs.

I'm so grateful, she says, after.

I smile at her, not sure how to tell her that she shouldn't be.

Can I buy you dinner? she says.

I haven't eaten, and the kids are already in bed sleeping.

Sure, I say.

We agree to split a cheeseburger. She says she can never finish one all by herself and, though I'm starving, haven't eaten all day, I'm too thrilled by the suggested intimacy to refuse. She serves me, in a clutch, from her plate to mine, half of the French fries and we eat almost all of the food, not saying much, in not very long a time.

We talk at first about books and about teaching. I tell her I wanted to be an academic because books always made more sense to me than people, because words written down couldn't be refuted later on. I'm always shocked, I tell her, when I see students outside of class and have to talk to them about anything but whatever we've read together, when I have to make up the ideas and the questions from scratch.

She says she became a writer because it was the only space in which she ever had control.

I wrote about real people, she tells me. *Except I could do things to them, with them; I wasn't ineffectual in the face of whatever wants or needs they had.*

I forgot, she says, *that the actual people would still be there, and the same, when I was done.*

I like looking at her as she talks. We sit at a small table, in chairs with caned backs and thin red cushions. I want to take my shoes off, to pull my knees up to my chest. The tables are close to one another and when people get up on either side of us they have to hold their coats and bags up over their heads so they don't brush against us as they walk past. The lighting's dim and the walls are red to match the cushions. There are booths along both back walls and worn movie posters hung behind the bar, the titles of which are all in French.

I used to listen to my drunk sister, she says, *on the phone for hours*.

She talked about her awful life, she says, *her bipolar, perennially out-of-work husband, her insane, drug-addled, Asperger's, ADHD kids.*

She chews a fry and smiles at me. *I took notes*, she says.

I eat the last bite of my cheeseburger. It's too big a bite and I hold my hand over my mouth as she waits for me to speak and then goes on.

I always asked her, she says, *if I could use it*. *Carla*, I said, *I'm going to use this in my work; is that okay?*

The Chilean writer looks past me through the window to the street, where students walk past in clusters, where cabs and large, dark SUVs drive by.

She said yes every time, but she was drunk.

The waiter brings a second round of beers and I hold my thumb over the lip, not eager to drink it. I don't like beer, really, but when she mentioned that the beer list looked good, I wanted to be like her, so I ordered what she got.

She killed herself, says the Chilean writer.

She sips her beer then and I sip mine right after.

I haven't written about it yet, she says.

That weekend, I sleep past six. I lie up in bed as my husband makes the children breakfast, reminds them to use the bathroom, asks them if they want to help him knead the biscuits. I'm awake, but I pretend that I'm asleep so I can stay in bed a while longer and just listen. I climb down when he calls to me to say that breakfast is ready and we eat together before he leaves for work.

Don't forget the birthday party, he says before he leaves, and I say, *Oh, fuck* before realizing the kids are right there watching and both of them look up and smile at me. The four-year-old whispers something to her sister and they laugh and run into their room.

We have no present for the birthday party and we have no time to buy one, so I have the children pick two books that they don't like much and a toy they haven't played with in a while and we make wrapping paper out of computer paper by drawing pictures on it and we wrap all of it up using a stapler because we don't have tape.

As soon as we walk into the ground floor of the brownstone, the four-year-old says loudly to the mother of the child whose birthday we're attending, *My mom didn't have time to get a gift so she made us wrap up our own toys.*

I look down and smile and walk past this woman toward

the back of the house while the kids head into the main room, where a TV that covers almost the whole wall plays a loud cartoon and children climb overtop piles of toys and squeal and scream.

There are bloody marys in the kitchen, says another mother.

It's eleven in the morning.

Great, I say.

In the kitchen sit seven other mothers and the father of the child whose party this is. He mixes bloody marys, all the ingredients set before him, half-empty jars of olives and tiny onions. He pours one out for each of us, taste-testing, dipping a finger in each glass and licking before handing us our drinks.

There's this Korean place, though, says one of the women. I've come in midconversation and they seem to be comparing places where they go to seek self-care. *They cover you in this thick, salty mud, then spray it off of you with this incredibly strong hose.*

It doesn't hurt, though?

It feels amazing. I mean, it sort of hurts, but, like, good *hurts*, she says. *Like waterboarding the dead skin.*

I go to the Russian baths in Queens, another woman says.

There's a sensory deprivation tank in Carroll Gardens, says a woman who wears the softest-looking turtleneck I've ever seen. *It's, like, two hundred dollars for forty minutes, but you leave feeling like you've come fresh from someone's womb.*

Botox, says another woman, reddening a little. *I'm almost forty*, she says. *I got this chemical peel a couple of weeks ago.* She makes a high-pitched sound that might be meant to be a laugh and reaches her hand up to her cheek. *I feel better when I like the way I look*, she says.

This fucking world, though, says another woman. *We have to do what we can.*

Klonopin, says another woman. *Xanax and weed.*

What I really want, though, says the only woman who has not spoken up until now. She sits on a stool in the corner of the room and has already sucked down to just the ice of her bloody mary. She is very thin and wears a blue silk shirt and her dark hair is pulled back from her face. *I don't want to talk,* she says, *or think. I want to stay standing with my shirt and shoes on and my pants around my ankles and a curtain held in front of my face and I want a strange man that I have never met and never have to meet to fuck me hard and then I want to leave.*

The next morning, which is the morning before we go to court to declare ourselves bankrupt, I wake up early, even though it's still the weekend, and I run fifteen miles into Manhattan and back home over the bridge. The sidewalks are still covered in ice and I fall three times and scrape my palms through my gloves and when my husband sees them, bruised and bloody, as I peel off all my clothes and climb into the shower, I look at him and say, *Self-care,* and he laughs.

I dress up for bankruptcy court and then wonder if I shouldn't wear something cheaper looking. Just before the magic credit card stopped working I went to the store I like the most in the West Village, a store I had never been inside of because it looked too expensive, and bought the shirt and pants I'm wearing now. We are, the lawyer told us, when we met with him the first time—when we finally had the two thousand dollars cash we had to pay him to declare officially that we had no money—great candidates for bankruptcy.

What is this supposed to feel like? I ask my husband.

Relief? he says.

He stands close to me in our bedroom, halfway beneath our bed, before we leave, and he is big and tall and I feel better.

Failure? he says. *An end?*

We drop the kids at school together for the first time in a long time. I feel grateful to get to do this. I kiss them, hold them. I let each of them lead me around the rooms where I have never been and where they spend every day.

We should go to court more often, I whisper to my husband.

He smiles at me, tired looking. He kisses each girl on the cheek.

It's mostly mothers, waving, saying goodbye. My husband waves or nods to all the mothers; they smile at him, hands reaching for their hair or clothes or for their children if they're close to them. They look at me warily.

While we wait for my husband to come back from the bathroom, on a bench outside the room that we will soon enter, where we will sit and wait again in different chairs, the bankruptcy lawyer mentions quietly to me that he majored in literature.

I wanted to be a writer, he says. *An academic.* He says this last word like it's magic, like this is not really a thing a person is.

I smile, my thumb rubbing the soft corner of this shirt that I won't ever pay for.

Dodged a bullet there, I say.

The first time I got pregnant it was an accident. I didn't believe that it was real until I took a digital test, alone, in the bathroom of a coffee shop I used to go to when I was twenty-one. I didn't believe it before I saw the word, but, though I'd imagined maybe I'd at least float the idea that we not have her, though I'd never before that been sure I wanted kids—I knew we were too broke to have her; I was still in grad school—I ached for her as soon as I saw that word form. I had an emergency C-section, and my student health insurance didn't cover C-sections—or, it covered C-sections, but only partially. We owed the hospital thirty thousand dollars, and then I was up all night nursing and walking the baby up and down the hallway and eating handfuls of chocolate chips to stay awake and then never remembering to rebrush my teeth. I got two root canals and one of them abscessed and the tooth had to be removed and they said that if I didn't get the tooth replaced my jaw would slowly collapse and I got a ten-thousand-dollar manmade tooth and another crown. We got too much takeout because we were both working and trying not to pay for childcare. My husband still owed more than a hundred grand in student loans from undergrad. I kept buying things: another breast pump because of the chafing with the first one, creams and ointments and sleep sacks and a noise machine and different types of swaddling blankets and a dehumidifier, in hopes that I could get the baby—the first baby, and then the second baby less than two years later—to finally go to sleep.

My body almost single-handedly bankrupted us. It also, with a little bit of help, made and then sustained the two best things in our lives. We were just privileged enough to think that we could live outside the systems and the structures and survive it, but we failed.

I think that there will be court but there is not court. There is a small, windowless room and those sad not-fold-out-but-also-not-quite-sturdy-or-comfortable industrial rows of chairs. There are eight of us there for the 10:30 am appointment. Six of us are clients of the same lawyer. Before we're brought into that room that is the main room, he brings us into a similar room and prepares us all at once. The lawyer is Korean and three of his other clients are Korean, so he tells us the directions once in English, then he says them again in Korean.

We all nod, and then, one by one, he talks to us about our case. He ushers us all out, then calls us back in one by one.

You guys will be fine, he says, looking at us, smiling. He's forty-something. He has this boyish, thick, dark hair that he has to sweep out of his face as he speaks. I wonder if he thinks it's somehow cool or if he just never remembers that he needs to get it cut.

You sure you don't stand to inherit any money in the next year? he says.

We look at one another, my husband and I; we shake our heads. This is not the first time he's asked this question. *We're sure*, I say.

And you don't currently have anyone that you might sue, from whom you might stand to get a settlement? Any type of personal injury?

We look again at each other, though he has also already asked us this.

Sure, we say. *No.*

You guys are all set, he says.

We wait a beat too long and he has to nod toward the door, motion to us to exit, so he can take the next Korean guy.

We wait outside and the guy next to us asks us the ages of our children. *I have four*, he says, *but they live with their mother. Expensive little fucks*, he says, and laughs. He wears jeans and work boots. I am the only female in the room. I feel overdressed.

When we enter the last room, the room in which we will actually be questioned, I keep thinking we are going to get in trouble. I don't have my phone because they made us hand them over after walking through the metal detectors. This whole building is for people going bankrupt, so, though I've gotten so dressed up, the security guards all know why we are there. I am convinced the school will call and I won't be there to answer; I'm unsure how we will explain that we were in bankruptcy court and therefore could not come to pick up our sick kids.

The men who speak Korean go first. They call a translation service on the phone and ask to be patched through to a Korean translator.

That's cool, whispers my husband.

I feel like we're not supposed to think anything is cool right now, but I nod.

The first two cases are straightforward. The woman who asks the questions is middle in the way women are often middle: age and weight and height. Nondescript in all ways. Her voice stays at the same tone as she asks her questions and at the end she says, *Good luck to you,* in a way that both feels scripted and, I hope, only feels scripted because she says it every day, to everyone. She has a long face and a long nose and stringy blond hair that looks greasier than it should this early in the morning, but then the lighting in this room is awful, and she must spend so much of her time inside.

I pity her for this and for this job with all these people and their failures. I am one of these people with these failures, but still, I'm glad that I'm not her.

With the last Korean man—he lost a deli that he'd opened in Midtown with a partner—the logistics are more complicated. Another lawyer is there to contest his bankruptcy, a lawyer from the bank that gave him a second mortgage on his house on Long Island. The other lawyer is young and thin and wears an oddly fitting suit. We all lean forward as the woman asks more questions than she's asked before this, as she lists the sums, which are bigger than the sums we've heard before.

Our lawyer, who is also this man's lawyer, puts his forearms on the stack of papers he's set before him and nods solemnly as the other lawyer talks.

You own a house, though? asks the middle woman.

He borrowed 1.6 million dollars against his mortgage to open up this salad bar and deli, except it didn't work.

What kind of shape is the house in? the man who has come to represent the bank says.

Bad, says the man who borrowed all that money. *Real old, real bad,* he says. He shakes his head.

He keeps speaking English, even though he asked for the translator; he answers the questions before they've been translated. The lawyer keeps telling him to wait, but he keeps interrupting. The man from the bank is young and can't stop fidgeting. His knee shakes up down up down underneath the table. He has a legal pad he writes on, a large scrawl; circles and squares around specific questions. He takes notes as the man talks.

You can send more questions to my office, says our lawyer. *We can answer all these questions for you in writing at a later date.*

The bank lawyer nods at our lawyer but keeps looking at the man who looks at the speaker where the translator sits, quiet now that she's stopped trying.

Is your wife's name on the deed? asks the bank lawyer.

She hate me, says the man. *She want divorce.*

When it's our turn we sit in the chairs and the woman asks us to say our names and to show her our IDs and to confirm we live at the address on the forms she shows us. She asks half the questions the lawyer told us she would ask us. Then our lawyer is ushering us out of the chairs and then out of the room and then we are outside and my husband says we should go eat before I go back to work.

We declared bankruptcy today, I text Sasha. I text this to my parents also, who have a lot of money. They have a lot of money but a few months ago, when I told my dad the state that we were in and that we needed help—though I hadn't asked for help before and for a long time I said fuck them and their fucking money and was angry and was mean—he told me that giving me money would be like throwing it away.

Neither of them responds to me, not Sasha, not my parents. The next day, while I'm staring at a young woman who is wearing too much makeup on the subway on my way to work, my dad texts to say, *I know how hard it must have been*. My mom texts an hour later: *It will all be fine, I'm sure*.

I wonder if any family, after too long trying and failing to love one another, can hear one another's words beyond all the ways that they fall short.

I'm pregnant, Sasha texts at two in the morning.

I wonder if she meant to send this to me, if she sent it like I sent the one on her birthday: not quite knowing what I was doing. I sent it because I needed her to remember that I was still somewhere in the world.

It was hot already, wet and sticky—college; I was nineteen; she was twenty; she'd driven from her school three hours away to spend the summer with me—and she shaved my head out on the roof of the row house I shared with two other girls and laughed as large chunks of hair fell down to the porch; the buzz of her hands on my neck was the closest that I'd come to joy in years. For weeks, we'd talked about it, a joke I made that she latched onto. I liked the thrill she seemed to get at the prospect: a sort of recklessness I'd receded from—mostly, then, I was locked up in my attic room—just as hers was amping up.

I didn't think I'd care what I looked like after. I had images of waiflike women with large features staring back at me from pictures, pictures that I'd found online when we first discussed shaving my head. I must have cared if I searched this. I must have been invested in how it'd turn out in the end. These women were all barefaced as well as bareheaded: Sinéad O'Connor, cancer victims, Yael Stone. All of them wide-eyed toward the camera. All of them gaunt. Their features threatened from their faces, big and unprotected, unapologetic; it was the viewer, though, who seemed to need protecting then.

That my features were too small and my face already too wide and blunt was not something I'd considered. That I'd gained weight and what was, would always be, too soft had gotten softer was something I tried not to think about. But then the hair had fallen to the porch and we were sweeping it into the trash and there was nothing to be done but to wear skullcaps in the wet summer heat and try to forget it was possible that I was making passers-by afraid.

I didn't mind because she loved me like that. She loved me most when, at night, she'd rub my back as I cried about whatever small thing made me cry that day and she could tell me my crying was allowed and important, that she'd be there no matter what. She reached her hands over the nubs of my head, strong and sure and doting, she talked and talked, until I fell asleep.

Men sought her out, always. I was an obstacle they had to overcome. They pretended to care about what I was reading so she would see that they were kind and thoughtful. They would half listen to the things I said as they turned their chairs closer to her. We both brought books to the same bar every night—it was the summer I read all of Woolf and Faulkner—the presence of the absence, circling, circling but not ever touching, knowing that there was no such thing as saying just exactly what one wanted, no such thing as connecting wholly with another human, but still trying anyway. She sometimes picked up whatever I had finished so we could talk about them afterward. The bar was Irish. They served colcannon and champ, boxty, boiled bacon and cabbage, and we'd split a big, hot meal after not eating the whole day. It was half old men, locals, and half undergrads who wanted to declare themselves as different from the kids who went to the fancy burger place or the oyster bar down the street.

I read and she held the books close to her, unopened, flirting with the bartender or pretending not to notice when men looked. I nodded and sometimes let myself pretend these men were interested in my answers to their questions. When they circled their chairs to face only her, I went back to my book. It was the contrast that never failed to shock me. We felt so much aligned during the day, at home, alone, walking down the street. We were the same age, from the same place, equally unrelenting, depressive, bookish. But the shape of her face, the way clothes hung on her body, her perfect skin, the largeness of her eyes: we were such completely separate things.

She came home with me almost always. When we made fun of these men later, the experience of their desperate want felt shared. It was mine insofar as I had gotten what they wanted. One of them called me a dyke bitch when I asked her if we could please go home after he offered to pay for her fifth beer. This one was attractive. Smart. It was 2:00 am. I'd read an entire novel in the time we'd been there. Probably she would have slept with him if I'd not made my face so sad when I'd asked if we could leave. If she'd not also heard what he'd said.

During the day, I could forget about this. My roommates both went back to their childhood homes and we had the whole place to ourselves for the last month. We'd get up early and walk over the MIT bridge into Boston. We wore T-shirts and sports bras, cotton shorts and flip-flops, just like we'd done all those years at home. There was a tree outside the house where I lived and we would pick mulberries to eat from our hands and pockets on our walks. We'd stop in Central Square for coffee. She'd get chocolate cake but never finish it. I'd get a quiche and then she'd pass me what was left of her cake. We drank cup after cup of coffee. Still there was the talking. Talking, talking. About the books that we were reading, about what we wanted, needed, thought then that we couldn't live without. I imagine now that it sounded and was shaped like what lots of young girls say they want and need when they're nineteen and twenty. She wanted always to be loved and wanted. I wanted to be anything but whatever I was then. We loitered on the basement floors of used bookstores when it got too hot and we were tired. We got ice cream on Newbury

Street and watched the tourists yelling, pointing in the duck boats on the Charles. We went to see movies; sometimes we snuck piles of food into our bags and stayed for hours, leaving one theater and sneaking into another. We'd see three or four films in six hours, stumbling out bleary and exhausted, the whole day having passed. I'd forget then, on the best days, that we were separate. Our words and wants and limbs would overlap. A man came up to our table at the coffee shop and dropped her a note, a pencil-sketched picture of her, *I just couldn't stop looking*, he wrote at the bottom, already gone. Three of the baristas asked her out. I'd gained weight, stopped running for long stretches of time, and none of my shorts fit. My head was still bare and sometimes people gawked, but mostly I could disappear inside reading and talking. I bought more cotton shorts and wore old, large sweat shirts with the sleeves rolled up.

I was paying for her. My parents paid. She was staying in my attic apartment until she *found a place*, except she never looked. She was meant to get a job but never did. We put our whole lives on the card I had, had always had, for living. She alluded sometimes to feeling bad about this, but I demurred and didn't let her talk too much about it. I didn't want to spend long stretches of time without her. The rent had to be paid regardless and she ate so little. At night, her drinks were always bought by men.

One night, we went out to dinner. I wore a green cotton strapless dress I'd had since high school that had seemed to fit in the dark apartment but did not. She wore a low-cut black silk tank and perfect pants. The busboy kept coming over to refill our waters. Even when I stopped drinking mine, to get him to stop, he found reasons, changing out our silverware, refolding her napkin when it fell off her lap. He was boorishly attractive, younger than us, broad-shouldered, dark hair, shockingly blue eyes. She pretended not to notice through the first course. But we spent every day together, every night and morning. We talked about the same things over and over. I saw her turn her body toward him. She let him look at her. When he finally spoke, his accent was South Boston born and bred. *You want more bread?*

He left her a note, scratchy handwriting, a pen borrowed from a waiter; he'd written his number and the word "drink" with a question mark. I was still hoping we could laugh about this later. I was still thinking if I ignored him she would too. *It'll be fun,* she said. *We'll go together.* I didn't want to. The energy was different between them than with most of the others. I could feel her *wanting* him to look at her, instead of acquiescing to it; I already understood I wouldn't be able to convince her not to go. I wanted to scream and cry and wrap both of us inside the tablecloth until we were home and no one could touch us with their eyes or food or drinks or pens or hands. *I want to go home,* I said. *Fine,* she said. Her voice was hard.

I left and she didn't. He dropped her off at my apartment the next day before noon. For weeks, she disappeared for days to be with him. I always knew where she was at night if she wasn't across from me in bed.

She made fun of him in front of me. *His sheets,* she said. Her face scrunched up. *I'm not sure they've ever been washed.*

She was affecting this not caring. She tried to convince me I still mattered most of all. He'd dropped out of high school, lived with a cousin in South Boston, no real plans. She said when he fucked her he got angry just before he came and she liked the way his ass felt in her hands, taut and small compared to the rest of him. Twice, she showed me bruises he'd left across her body. I ran my hands slowly over them, one on the shoulder, another just below her chin, her skin so white and poreless, even in summer, the purple splotches popping, angry, with smaller patches of brown and blue. Later, I reached slowly up into myself with that same hand and let myself remember her pulse thrumming; I thought about their fucking, imagined the feel of that hard, angry ass overtop of me.

He stopped returning her calls after a month. She pretended she didn't care. Then she told me she thought she might be pregnant. She refused to take a test but left a message on his phone. I went to the CVS and bought the test for her, but she refused to take it. Instead, she curled up next to me in my bed and cried, her phone clutched to her. When he still hadn't called her back a week later and she was still calling, warning, saying she'd take care of it herself except she didn't have the money now (I knew this wasn't true and had also offered to put an abortion on my parents' credit card) I found a used tampon in the bathroom under two sheets of paper from the day's news. We were the only people in the house.

I CALL IN sick to work and meet the Chilean writer for breakfast at a diner in the Village. It's the end of the month and we've just paid our rent and made the girls' school payment and the magic credit card no longer works. I realize, halfway through breakfast, that I can't afford this meal.

I can't pay for this, I say out loud, scared all of a sudden.

The Chilean writer sits up very straight and smiles at me. Her books have never sold too well in the States, but she has a reputation overseas.

I can, she says.

We were different types of objects, I say, as I tell her about Sasha.

She appeared and I didn't, I say. *I didn't wholly understand then, how limited her power was. I didn't understand how contingent her power was on other people wanting her.*

And you? she says. *Your wants?*

She wears glasses and has large eyes that are made larger by the glasses. The glasses' frames are wide and round and black and overwhelm her face.

I know now all the ways not being looked at kept me safe.

Our server refills our waters. In the time that we've been here, the place has filled, then emptied. I don't know why I'm talking about her. It was a whole other life. I want this not to be the same story of this friend I loved and how I lost her. I want to be past whatever it was I thought I got away from when I left Florida all those years ago.

I wasn't in the world, I say. *I was detached from almost everyone but her.*

Not without its dangers, she says.

Sure, I say. *But self-inflicted dangers are a different thing.*

I get seven emails from work in the time we sit and nurse coffee after coffee. The twenty-four-year-old couldn't find the readings he was meant to give the students, so he let them watch a movie, and my co–homeroom teachers had to defuse a fight after lunch between two of the kids I teach. My husband texts to ask about my day at work and I text back and say it's fine and ask how his is.

On my walk home from all that coffee, I text Sasha. *Congrats*, I say, after hours of not responding. She does not, of course, respond, and I feel dumb.

3

My alarm goes off and I climb down the stairs of our bed, grab my phone, and turn it off and stuff my phone underneath my pillow. I close my eyes again. I reset the alarm for 5:00 and then 5:30. My calves and neck hurt, my lower back. My husband's still asleep and I crawl to the middle of the bed and bend my knees, my ass against my calves. I stretch my arms up to the front of the bed and press my forehead hard against the sheets and breathe slowly in and out.

I run four miles instead of eight and am rushed and anxious after. Our four-year-old has wet the bed and the two-year-old is crying, holding on to all my limbs, screaming that she hates my job, that she wants me to stay with her, pulling on my sweater to wipe the snot off her nose and lips and chin.

I have to go to work, I tell her. *People have to go to work*, I tell her. *So they can live.*

Just go, my husband says, packing their lunches, making breakfast, cleaning up the four-year-old in the bathtub, changing her sheets. *Let go of your mother*, he says to the baby.

I want to come to work with you, she says. *Nurse*, she says.

You have to go, says my husband.

I hold the two-year-old another minute, wiping her face with my sweater, reminding her to breathe.

I'll see you tonight, I tell her. This isn't true, though, I remember just after I say this. It's Thursday and I won't be home until long after she's asleep. I try not to do this, tell them I will be somewhere when I won't be. I try not to ever promise things to them that I can't give. But it's too late now and I have to go and she won't stop crying.

The four-year-old is still not wearing any pants and she comes out of her room and I pick her up to find her underwear and leggings, still holding the baby. *You're going to be late,* says my husband. I dress the four-year-old and kiss her, hug her, give the red-faced baby to my husband. I hug them one more time and miss my train.

I have been called into a meeting with the principal and wonder briefly if the twenty-four-year-old has reported me. I've been leaving at least twice a week. I don't think anybody sees me, but I also don't work very hard to keep my leaving a secret. I walk out with my bag and coat on, usually while classes are going on so there aren't many people in the hallways. When I pass coworkers, I assume they think I'm going out for coffee or a late lunch. Twice, the twenty-four-year-old has messaged me on the Google chat when I've been on the subway or already back in Brooklyn, and I've made things up about my kids.

Three times, I've had to ask my co–homeroom teachers to cover for me. I blame my children. I lie to my co–homeroom teachers because they're just as frustrated with this job as I am but they don't leave.

I see the twenty-four-year-old lingering, close to the principal's office, just before I'm led in by his admin assistant. I brace myself for the look I'll get at home when I tell my husband I lost this job and it's my fault. I imagine what response I might give to excuse it, but I leave because I want to, which is not, I think, a reason I should say out loud to try to keep my job.

The principal appears, though, not to know about my midday leaving. Instead, he explains calmly to me that it's time for test prep, that the portion of the year in which the kids are meant to be doing anything but test prep has long since passed. I am not, he tells me, trained in test prep and so will no longer be teaching the students I've been teaching since the fall.

I remind him I spent years as a test-prep tutor.

But you haven't been trained by us, he says.

The teachers who they're bringing in are coming from the middle school.

Middle school? I say, obviously disdainful.

You're not being generous, he says to me.

I'm not.

He eats the whole time we talk, hot soup with a hulking piece of bread that he dunks into the soup and then into his mouth. He sits back in his chair, his ankle on his knee, and each time I talk he smiles.

But they're learning, I say.

I realize that I might start crying, but I refuse to cry in front of this man whom I think of as a child.

He tells me that this was not his decision. *The network*, he says, smiling. *Nothing I could do.*

I love my students and am sad and angry, even though I know I leave sometimes for no good reason and that makes my love for them questionable at best. I tell my boss I think this is the wrong decision, and he stares blankly at me and doesn't speak. He takes a bite of his bread and a clump lands briefly on his chin. We both pretend that I'm not crying. With all the things I hate about this job, the students are the only reason that I stay.

Teaching, I say, *is ninety percent buy-in.*

He nods.

They're bought in, I say.

I try to tell him that they're thinking and that they've been enjoying thinking. I try to tell him that he told me when he brought me on that he cared about helping them think.

He tells me he is grateful for my *investment in the children and the vision*. I will teach different kids now, kids who, he says, also need me—kids upon whom, I think, they have already given up. I'll teach the seniors, who have already gotten into college or they haven't, who have already taken all the tests there are to take.

I'm no longer crying, and I smile at him. I imagine he thinks I'm smiling because he's managed to convince me of this plan I don't agree with, but really he has spilled soup on his shirt and tie and, the way his face looks anxious and earnest at once now that he's trying to convince me that everything is fine, he reminds me of a kid in our daughter's pre-K class whose toes she stepped on while they stood in line for lunch because, she told me later, she did not know how else to make him be quiet like the teacher asked.

I leave the principal's office and have to do my hall duty. Hall duty means sitting at a table in the hall as students walk back and forth between the bathroom and class. Sometimes students stop to talk or flirt and I have to tell them to move on. The ones who know me loiter and we talk about the classes that they're taking, the social dramas that I know of. I'm trusted as much as the most trusted white teachers, which is to say kindly, generously, joking often—but also warily.

Twenty minutes in, the chat says that Kayla's missing. I check the third-floor bathroom and see her shoes, the toes turned in again.

Kayla? I say.

She's in the large handicap accessible stall and opens up the door and motions for me to come inside. I look back and forth, not sure if I'm supposed to do this or if I care if I'm supposed to do this. I'm not super invested, in this moment, in keeping my job.

You okay? I say.

She nods again for me to come in with her. There's a bandage around her arm and it has slipped.

I come through the door and she locks it behind me. I sit down on the floor next to her. *Are you okay?*

She nods.

What's this?

She tells me that her mother saw the bruise on her face from where her boyfriend hit her and when she told her what had happened, her mother took her to a doctor and had a birth control device implanted in her arm.

I hit him back, though, she says. *My mother lets men put their hands on her, but he won't do it to me again.*

May I? I say, nodding to her arm.

I unwrap the bandage slowly and roll it in my hands. I hold it up above the mark where the device has been implanted and I slowly wrap it, asking, with each rotation, if the pressure is too tight.

Fine, she says each time, so I keep it extra tight, watching her face.

Okay? I ask, when I have finished.

Fine, she says another time.

I text the Chilean writer three days in a row and she doesn't answer and I get frantic. I call her and I email and I'm afraid both that she is not okay in some bodily unsafe way and also that I've accidentally scared her off. *I'm so sorry*, she emails on the fifth day. *My son was in town and we got busy. Everything all right?*

The next Thursday, I leave work early because I leave early even more now; he's taken my students from me and, I figure, if I'm caught now, I'll have something to say.

I go up to the campus where I teach my night class. I'm early and am hoping to find an empty office where I can read. In the small café, at the foot of the stairs, leading up to the department offices, I see the girl who emailed, weeks ago, asking to meet.

Kate, I say, grabbing her arm. *Honey*, I say, more like a mom than I meant. *We never met*.

She reddens—on her shoulders, bare like always, on her round cheeks.

It's not a big deal, she says.

She's with friends, a thin boy with too-big glasses and a tall, dark girl I've never seen. They look back and forth between us. I'm often mistaken for a student, not because I look so young but because I don't assert much authority, because no one knows who I am or why I'm there. I slip in and out and teach my class and am not around besides that, because I'm not sure why anyone would or should listen when I speak. I felt the same when I was a student at this vaunted institution, like I didn't quite deserve it, like any minute, someone would come and ask me to leave.

Come up, I say to Kate. *I'm getting an office; come with me.*

She looks at her friends and the small boy looks down at his shoes.

Come catch me up, I say.

She has a coat slung over her arm and a big bag that she drapes across her body. There's something sloppy about her that I admire, not unlike Sasha. She's always seemed to take up space unapologetically.

I ask the kids behind the desk for an office, though I'm early. I tell them that I'm sorry. For the first hour that I'm required to hold office hours, I am in one office, then someone with tenure takes that office over and I'm switched to a smaller one with random extra chairs piled in the back for the remaining hour.

Either of them free? I say.

The girl who always makes my copies and who is always kind smiles, gets up. She was a lawyer before this.

413, she says. This is the bigger office, without broken chairs. I smile at her, grateful.

What's up? I say, when the door's closed and this girl has slung her coat across the seat, her bag still hung across her chest and on her lap in a heap.

You know, she says. *Busy.*

Her skin begins to splotch again and I wonder if she's even younger than I think, teenaged, some sort of prodigy.

You wanted to talk? I say.

It's nothing, she says. *I wanted. This weird thing happened the other day.*

Okay . . . I say.

She tells me she was at a party with other students from the program.

I was drunk, she says, and looks down at her bag, still in her lap.

Okay . . . I say.

I was talking to this guy, she says. *And he asked me about my dissertation advisor, about what I study. I told him, and he told me he had this guy I'd heard about.*

She says: *I'd heard about,* like it holds within it more than the words mean.

She says: *I told him I'd heard he was an ass to girls.*

Okay . . . I say.

It's just . . . Her shoulders are red again and she grabs hold of the hair behind her ears and starts to twist it.

I heard the guy was creepy, and I told him, she says. *And he told me that wasn't a thing, that he's sort of a flirt but it's all fine because the guy has a kid.*

I laugh then, though probably I shouldn't.

The office that we're in is small and the books on the shelf behind her were all written by another, much older man who teaches here, who has tenure, who isn't ever here.

I was just so pissed off, she says. *Like he didn't care, you know? Like a guy being an asshole to girls is fine with him.*

I both do and don't know. She's ten years younger than me and, if this were me, *when* this was me, if I had spoken to this guy, I would have thought about it for weeks, for months, but I would not ever have recounted the cxperience out loud to someone else. I would have decided not to like this guy right after. I would have noted to myself that we would not be friends. I would have been quietly embarrassed by my sensitivity and discomfort. I would have felt very small and very sad throughout.

I tried to push him on it, she says. *And he shut me down.*

She is doughy, sweet and soft, and I want to tell her

everything will be okay and to just not think about this. I don't want to be one more person telling her what she says doesn't matter, but I'm also not sure it does.

I called a friend of mine who goes to another college where he used to adjunct. She says her friend's friend said he tried to kiss her during office hours.

Another of their friends was his babysitter, she says. *And he tried to kiss her too. Asshole*, she says, more to herself than me.

I think I'm supposed to only listen, but she's stopped talking now and looks at me.

That sucks, I say.

I don't want to tell her it's expected. I don't want to tell her that this is how things are, although it is.

It's tricky, I say.

This was wrong, and I almost tell her that I'm sorry.

My friend says, she says, *he shouldn't be allowed to teach*.

Can I help? I say. *Do you want to tell me his name?*

She says it and I think a minute and then place him, his perfectly shaven face, his short, squat frame. This man has health insurance from this job—a temporary appointment, but more solid than my own, and I wonder briefly if this is how I might take his job from him.

He didn't do anything to me, she says. *I've never talked to him*.

I think of all the stories that I heard when I was a grad student, how we only ever whispered about them later, how embarrassed I was that none of them belonged to me.

Do you know anyone who has experience of this firsthand? I say.

The women in his class don't like him.

I'm not sure— I say.

Never mind, she says.

I don't want— I start.

How can I help? I say.

I just wanted to say to someone how awful it feels.

It sucks, I say, for the three thousandth time.

Why did that kid think it was okay?

I don't know, I say.

If someone that you know knows more, you guys should tell someone, I say.

She nods, her shoulders red, folding her coat on her lap, waiting for me.

I am someone she has told.

Let me think about this, I say. *Email me,* I say, *if there's any way at all you think that I might help.*

After my class, I find Melissa, who is older, whip smart, head of the department. She somehow willed herself into this job, which feels miraculous still now. She gave me this job. Each semester, I email to ask her if I can teach the next semester, and each semester she gets right back to me and says *Yes, of course; I'll find something.*

Come in, she says. She's always here. She holds extended office hours always. When I was a student here I came to see her once a week.

How's class? she says.

I want to tell her about the thing with my student, but I'm not sure what I'd say, what there even is to tell her.

I'm tired, I say.

They need so much, she says.

I think of all the emails that I wrote her when I was a student, asking her for coffee, but really, asking her to tell me I could do this, it was worth it, I was special, everything would be okay.

How are you? I say to her. I think about how I've maybe never asked her this and how awful I've been for not asking. I've asked her this, but never wanted or expected a response.

She smiles. She has a thin-lipped, wry, large-eyes-closing-at-the-corners smile.

She has red, curly hair, tied up, but loose, random wisps around her face.

She looks down at her hands. Her fingernails are dark blue and she has a large black opal ring on her right middle finger. She wears a dark blue turtleneck and black pants. She smiles again, but this time her lips fold in toward her teeth.

When she looks up the smile's gone.

My fucking dog is dying, she says.

I cross my legs and clasp my hands around my knee. *I'm sorry,* I say.

She shakes her head.

You're the first person today to ask me how I am, so now you're paying for it. She's twenty, she says. *Old,* she says. *Ancient for a dog.* She looks at me and lets out a sort of laugh. *I understand that she's a dog and I'm not supposed to be so sad.*

She works harder than any other person in this program. She writes the most letters of recommendation, the longest comments on student papers, theses. The day I defended my dissertation she took me out for coffee and put her hand on my hand and told me she was proud of me.

She's the longest-lasting relationship I've ever had.

She's fifty-something, I think, maybe early sixties, never married.

She has cancer, she says, *arthritis. All the bad things,* she says and laughs again. *She's really fucking old.*

I still have my coat on and I unzip it slowly so she doesn't think I want to leave her.

The vet wanted me to put her down two weeks ago, she says.

She looks past me toward the door and I look out the window so she doesn't have to worry she might look me in the eye.

I'm torturing her because I can't fathom coming home and her not being there.

The next morning I sleep past my alarm again, but then run the distance that I want to run and then have to shower and change after the children are awake.

Mommy, yells the four-year-old as she stands in the bathroom and I shower. *Mommy,* she calls, *can you wipe?*

She has pooped and hates to wash her hands so always asks someone else to wipe so she can skip that step.

I lean out of the shower and get a piece of toilet paper and I wipe her. She kisses my wet cheek, then makes a face and stares at me, her face hard.

You're all wet, she says.

My mom calls early on that Sunday morning. It's the first I've heard from her since the bankruptcy. We haven't been to Florida since the four-year-old was a baby. Three months before our second baby was born, I told my parents we needed to stop talking, and they were hurt and sad.

Before that, for a long time, there was no talking without fighting. We'd get on the phone, and then I and whichever of them had gotten up the courage to try to call me would spend the whole time trying to win. We didn't know how to talk if it wasn't about winning: who knew better, who'd been hurt more and for longer, who'd tried harder when the other person didn't try at all. I was pregnant and already had a toddler and I was sick all of the time; I had four jobs. I told them that they needed not to call me for a while.

This is still fresh two years later. We didn't solve it. I had the baby and felt guilty. I sent them pictures of her the day after she was born. We slowly, gradually got back in touch. They're still mad. She calls, though, and she says they want to see us, *want to see the babies*. They haven't met the two-year-old. She offers to fly us down for the week of our spring break.

I don't want to say yes and know that it won't go well. My husband has work on Long Island and can't come. I think vaguely that they're my parents and I love them; I think maybe, if we're together with my babies, with the sunshine and the ocean, with them at work most of the time and me trying to be better, that maybe this time it won't all go as poorly as it has before.

There is no one story so much as lots of stories, a general way of being. There is not, in direct opposition to most of the books I read until I got to grad school, a clear cause and effect. There is we don't know how to talk to one another, the general feeling that we're all saying the right things, *trying*, except all of them are wrong. The general feeling that we think and say the same words, but they mean very different things to each of us.

My parents came from nothing and worked hard for their money, which also meant they thought anyone who was not also successful was not successful because they did not work hard enough. They loved us, tracked every grade and track meet, class rank and debate win, which also meant love was wrapped up tight with winning, that one's value was variable and contingent and could fall short at any point. Food was good but not-thin was disgusting. Flaws were fine but not ever when others might see. It was a world phantasmagoric with declarations for which one had to track and measure meaning, under which lived conditions, contradictions, a whole world of contingencies.

I was depressed is a clear, clean thing that I can say that might explain things. That my dad probably was too was not ever discussed. My whole life, I'd watched as he got sad and quiet and my mom yelled at him and he left the room and did not talk again for days. It was normal practice then for me to go into his room and beg him to come back, to come back out and ask my mom to please be nicer to him so he didn't throw another temper tantrum, to beg him later—when she yelled again and he walked out of the house, standing in the backyard, locking himself in the garage, pulling the car over so he could get out and walk along the highway—not to leave.

And then: I stopped showing up to track and stopped showing up to school and drank more. I got in three car accidents in four days my junior year of high school and was hospitalized for alcohol poisoning a few weeks after that. I refused to go to school and had to be withdrawn. I did not feel sick so much as I felt like I'd finally stopped doing what they wanted. I felt scared and tired and wholly out of control for a long time. None of this must have been easy to try to parent. Their reaction was half to not look directly at the aberrant child, to keep me hidden, half to lash out late at night when they didn't know what else to do.

He played victim; she got angry. *I might as well die if you don't love me*, he said to me. *You're a worthless piece of shit*, she said. *You're ungrateful and fucked up*. It was language that she'd thrown at him when I was little, that she gave me now.

They were scared and desperate; they yelled and threatened. I never knew if I was on their team or not. If I was, they would do anything, fight for me, defend me against coaches and teachers, take me to doctors, beg me to be better. If I wasn't, there was no end to what they'd hurl at me just to win, every error that I'd ever made but all in order, recorded and recast to show my failures in their clearest form. The worst part was always the not knowing. Not knowing if I might try again to love them, if any hint of needing, wanting, asking, would be held against me later on.

It was slippery linguistic manipulation, trying to find words but none of them quite working, *love me love me, not like that, just stop it. We love you, let us love you,* until it feels like every word holds its opposite inside it too. At least with hate you know what you are getting. Love like that, you forget sometimes it's not love, that it's empty, all words and performance, and still sometimes you grab at it, thinking maybe it will give what love's supposed to give.

I think now that if I met them on the street I would find them completely fine and bland, just people. I would find them stunted and a little sad. They wouldn't make me angry. It's only because they are the place where the word "love" was built for me that I feel such fury toward them, that each time I get too close, I get so mad.

At the airport my mom cries but no one talks about her crying. She picks up the baby and my father holds the four-year-old and I stand separate with the car seats and the stroller and our bags. I strap the car seats in my dad's Range Rover and my dad loads the bags and stroller in the back. He places the four-year-old into her seat, then asks if I can help him with the buckles, and my mother, having not let go of the baby since she saw us, settles her into the seat. We say as little as we can without ever stopping talking the whole half an hour that we're in the car together. They ask the children all the questions. I jump in to clarify or to restate the questions to the baby when she doesn't answer. I sit between them in their car seats and I hold tight to each of their hands and stare hard at the horizon—flat green marshland and rows of scrub trees, tall thin palm trees—so I don't puke or accidentally say something that I don't mean or scream.

We spend a week not really talking. Every night, when I can't sleep, I read Henry Green, *Party Going*—1939, a fog has fallen and a group of wealthy people meant to go on an excursion are trapped in a hotel together; an elderly aunt might be dying and there's drinking; a young woman takes a bath; the hotel staff pulls down the gates of the hotel and locks them, so that none of the people outside can get in.

The kids swim in the pool and at the beach and I go for long runs in the sand before they wake up. I run the same stretches of beach I've run my whole life, barefoot; I get blood blisters on the first couple of days, on my big toes and the balls of my feet, and I pop them and they harden over and the pain goes away. The water's warm and I take off my shirt and shorts and there are hardly any waves. My parents go to work each day. In the morning, before leaving, dressed in her suit, wearing the lotion that she's always worn to match her perfume, that I could smell three thousand miles away, my mom lays out cereals and fruit and bread and makes me a cup of coffee. She dotes on us. She's bought every food I've ever mentioned that the children might like: cheese and chicken, avocado, fig bars. The temperature inside the house is perfectly controlled.

We drop my mom at work so we can have her car to drive around, to go to the zoo, to get lunch. Three of the five days that we're there I drive my mom's car past Sasha's. Once, when the kids are both asleep and I'm just drained enough by the sun and weary, I almost pull into Sasha's parents' driveway before I remember she's not there.

I hardly shower the whole time we're there and stay salty all day, traipsing sand over my father's perfect floors while he stays quiet, mostly, wincing as our girls climb on the couch that I know no one sits on most of the time. He sits, usually with the TV on, while the children choose their cereal, while my mom makes dinner at night, while we all work not to fight.

I love Florida and I hate it. It's warm here even though it's still wet and cold in New York, and the beach goes on for miles with almost no one there. The stretch I run each morning is my favorite stretch of beach, my favorite stretch of land, maybe, in the world, so gorgeous and familiar, elemental to me; it's a thrill to share it with my girls. Every other part of this place, though, makes me anxious; my parents talking makes my body clench and I feel the children's bodies clench because mine is. They get worn out from the sun and throw tantrums. They can tell I'm not quite steady and they cling to me all day, crawl into bed with me at night.

I keep thinking I'll ask my parents for money. I think vaguely, when I said yes to coming, that this was why. I keep thinking: *Their house is so big,* and our older daughter keeps asking why they have so many bathrooms. It's lots of open space, dark wood, and blues and whites. They've gotten better over years at being wealthy. Neither of them grew up with money, but now they hire the right people to teach them how to spend what they have.

I was twenty-one when I told them that I did not want their fucking money. I was just out of college, stupid, privileged. What I was saying was *I dare you*. Try to find some way to love me in the way that I need loving. It was one of their favorite things to hold against me: my brand-new car and college education, the years that my sister and I got to ride horses on the weekends when we were small. I wanted them not to have this particular ammunition, to see what other forms of loving they might be up to instead.

What was most embarrassing was that when it came time to need, it was the thing I'd thought was not enough, it was their *fucking money*, that I wished that they would give to me.

Now, I want them to see my need, but I don't ask and they don't offer so instead I'm mean in small ways and then feel awful afterward.

They have to go to bed, Mom, I say, when she plans a movie night with my cousin and her children. *Don't make all that food,* I say, when she goes to cook an extra pound of fish. All she wants to do is cook them food and give them gifts and take their pictures so that she can post them on the internet. She wants to get some of the pictures printed and put into frames that match the frames that hold the pictures of my sister and me when we were children and put them on the mantel so she can look at them while she cooks dinner or gets dressed to go to work.

My father hardly speaks the whole time. There's a TV in every room and he watches CNBC. He looks scared when he looks at me, like the mess of me might somehow get on him and he won't ever be able to get clean.

Once, he asks about my job and I start to tell them but then my mother says, *Those kids are so lucky to have you,* and I look down at the food she's made me, then over at my children who've stopped eating and are playing, and I say, *No they're not, Mom,* and the three of us turn back toward the TV.

On the last day, my mother plays with our girls out on the porch. Both of them have come to love her. My father sits on his computer and I stay as still as I can in a corner of the couch. My mother pulls out all the toys that she's bought for the children and that we have no room for in our apartment—that I can't, by myself, carry back home on the plane.

We have to go soon, I say. They've gotten us a car to the airport.

My dad looks at his watch, and my parents look at one another.

Not yet, my father says. His ankle sits on his knee, and he opens up a file on his computer.

My mother's small eyes flit from my daughters to my father and back to me.

Watch this, my dad says. I move closer to him. *You have to watch this before you go,* he says.

His arms are crossed; so are my mother's. They're both attorneys. My whole life, their arms have been crossed.

He starts the video and there's laughing, yelling. It's me, my sister, my older cousin. I'm five or six, my sister two behind, my cousin two ahead. We're romping around the large house we lived in most of our early childhood. My uncle, who's visiting from far away, films. There's music playing and we're dancing. We're a little bratty, laughing, singing. We change our clothes. We romp and squeal. My little sister emulates our cousin, flapping her hair in front of her face and laughing, her nose close to the screen. I wear pigtails, the same pigtails I wore every day—my mother braided them, all dressed for work in heels and suit, black coffee, Estée Lauder lotion and perfume—straight up to middle school.

My father watches me—the grown-up me, not the one that's laughing, singing.

So, he says.

My mother watches too.

I know better than to talk right now.

This must be why you hate us? he says. *This part?*

We're still laughing. Five-year-old me has changed into a bathing suit and is running out to dive into the pool.

He says, *Is this the childhood that made you do such awful things to us?*

I want to ask them if they're serious. I want to stand up on this couch and yell and scream. There are twenty-nine years to fill the gap between this video and this day. *I don't—* I say, but then I stop. I can't tell him that you can't make a video of notness, that there's no way to record all the ways they weren't there.

This must be the part, my father says.

I dive into the pool on the screen.

Please, I say.

My mom stares at me: this must be the face she gives opposing counsel when she feels she's shut them down.

We have to go, I say.

My daughters look at me.

I've asked them not to do this when my girls are with me. I asked them to promise not to fight with me. They're not yelling now, though; they're just reminding me quietly, just by looking, of all that I've done wrong.

We're leaving, I say.

I pick up our two-year-old and she starts to scream. She arches her back. Her soft, round belly pops out from underneath her shirt.

My mother stands.

My father's ankle comes off his knee and his feet are even on the floor.

I grab hold of our four-year-old's hand.

She's fine, my mother says. The four-year-old looks at me, then her, then me. She keeps hold of my hand.

They follow us to the front door. We leave the toys and all the clothes my mother bought them. I have our two small bags. We sit, quiet, on the driveway and the baby nurses and the four-year-old flips through a book until the car comes to pick us up.

Coming home: the plane lands and I pull the bags out from the overhead compartment and the two-year-old cries most of the time because I can't hold her and our luggage and the four-year-old wets her pants as we get off the plane. Both of them want to sit in the fold-up stroller, so I put the four-year-old in first and then her sister on her lap and tell both of them to hold on tight; an old woman shakes her head at me, mutters loud enough so I can hear that I am being *reckless with those precious babies*, and it takes all the strength I have not to yell in her face. Out near the baggage claim, close to the exit, my husband, rumpled, no bag, coat unzipped and open, lets the children sit a minute longer, lets them fight about who gets to hug him first and roll out of the stroller onto the dirty airport carpet, takes all the bags off of my shoulders and puts them on the floor next to the children, arms around me, holds me, hugs me, whispers in my ear, *You're home*.

THERE'S BEEN A spring snowstorm and I've called in sick to my day job to attend a day of faculty development at the university.

It's a long message, almost a minute. I see it when I'm exiting the train. I get coffee from the coffee cart, milk and two scoops of sugar. I climb the stairs, which have gone icy, up to campus. The hand that doesn't hold my coffee clutches the cold rail. I take my left glove off to slide open my phone and listen to her voicemail. Her voice is shaky. She drives a convertible; I think I hear the wind around her in her car.

I just . . . she says. *Maybe it's the lawyer in me*, she says.

The cardboard cup is thin, and bends, the plastic cover comes undone and drops of coffee fall onto my coat. I've misplaced my winter boots and my feet are numb inside my leather shoes.

I pass a colleague, then another. I smile at them, nodding.

I'll do whatever you need me to, my mother says to my voicemail. *I'll come up there*. She's frantic. Her voice quavers. *I worry, though, about you. I talked to your father about maybe calling someone. I want to make sure.* She stops. I hear the wind and other cars driving past her. *What's most important*, says my mother, *is those little girls*.

I grab hold of the railing of the steps that lead to our department office as I almost slip.

I don't want you to lose your little girls, my mother says.

I'm standing in front of the building where we're meant to be meeting.

Colleagues pass me. I climb the six flights of stairs up to the auditorium to avoid talking in the elevator as I listen to the message two more times. I know what this is because it's happened once before this: they've suggested I'm not equipped to be a mother. She has. She has threatened to call authorities, *to check in*. This was just after I cut off contact. She has walked me through, via email and then in long voicemails on my phone and once my husband's, the various ways a child might be taken from a parent if the parent is not properly equipped. I've thought before this that these threats were empty. They don't, I tell myself, really think that my children should be taken from me. They just want me scared. Still, there is her voicemail here now and all the emails from two years ago that I have saved and pull up now on my phone.

Your little girls, my mother says, and I can see them, smell them, from this morning, sleep hair in their eyes and French-toast breath; I throw my coffee in a close-by trash can, worried I might throw it up.

I tap my pen through the first four hours of presentations. I slip my feet out of my shoes. I sit in back. I came in late and waved to my friends sitting together, walked up the steps to the last row so that no one would be behind me. They've brought in a guest lecturer to speak to us about arguments and Greeks. She's corpulent, short-haired, almost funny. She picks at her sweater, to keep it from tugging at her middle, as she speaks. She rubs her hand along the back of her neck and leans her head back when she loses hold of her train of thought. She makes self-deprecating jokes about herself that it's clear she only half believes.

Kronos, the speaker tells us, is time, chronology. *Topos is*, she says, *a place, any shared allotment of space*. She says we should tap into this idea when helping students learn. We should take them for walks, exploit their personal investment, explain to them their impact on *community*. Kairos is the sacred moment, the moment in which we learn or are introduced to an idea. She talks about how irrevocably our intellects attach themselves to time, knowledge that depends on where you are and whom you're with. She talks about reason a posteriori, in terms of the consequence after the fact.

I walk out of the large room with its stadium stairs and I replay the message standing in the hall. My socks are neon green and I curl my toes in. I want to scream into the phone. I want to yell at her to keep the fuck away. My hands shake and I do not want to reenter the auditorium. I've left my bag and my computer. I've yet to sign the sign-in sheet.

When I get back inside, the word "stasis" is in all caps on the board. Beneath it, the speaker's written "civil war." *In biology*, she says, *stasis is the moving of fluids back and forth. More hopeful definition*, she says, then she laughs. Second century BCE. Hermagoras. These were, according to him, the different forms arguments took inside a court of law. *Pre-lawyers*, she says. *Oft forgotten. Poor Hermagoras.* She laughs. She's taken off her sweater. The heat inside the room is stifling, thick. She wears a dark-blue short-sleeved shirt that pulls in places that suggest it was constructed for a man. She has a small vine tattoo that loops around her wrist, then spreads in thin intricate twists all up her arm. She wears glasses and pushes them up on her nose each time she writes on the board. She has a tiny speck of chalk on the left side of her cheek.

Five steps, she says, *make up the basic stasis questions. One: fact or conjecture. Everything is arguable*, she says, *maybe most of all the facts. Two: definition. Definitions*, she says, *are logotropic; definitions can trope, confine, recapitulate a whole argument. Three is quality or value—what sort of act is being argued, what it's worth. Four: cause or consequence. Five: procedure, proposal, policy—what should we do,* she says, *about whatever we're arguing? How do we find a way to move on?*

I go home and get our girls and somehow end up at my younger sister's. I do not like my younger sister. I think sometimes I would like my younger sister if we had not, our whole lives, been in a not-quite-clearly-constituted fight over who deserved to make it out intact.

She doesn't mean it, my sister says, on the too-hard loveseat my parents bought her. She never cut up their credit cards and now talks to them daily. They purchased and paid to renovate this apartment in Murray Hill. My girls laugh and play with a box of Q-tips that sits below my sister's vanity. They break them, then stick them in each other's noses.

For three years, most of college, my sister stopped eating almost completely and her bones began to turn to chalk and hair grew on her face, and I could still, now, loop my thumb and index finger around her wrists and they would meet.

You know how she is, my sister says. *She's just hurt,* she says.

My husband calls my sister *the apologist.*

She's not good at dealing with hurt, my sister says. *Tell them that you're sorry,* she says. *Let them think you think you're wrong.*

Before Dante gets on the boat in the Inferno, I tell my sister, *there are cries of anguish from the uncommitted—the souls who took no sides, those concerned not with good or bad but with how to take care of themselves. These people,* I tell my sister, *were naked and futile. They were stung relentlessly by wasps, fed on by maggots, in a sort of spiritual stagnation,* I say.

My sister looks at me, then at my girls, who have stopped with the Q-tips and are helping each other climb onto my sister's bed. She leans toward me, whispers to me—when she was little she used to threaten them, she used to tell them that if they yelled at her, if they made her practice her piano or come home at a certain time, she said, if they did that then she might turn out like me—she says: *Are you sure you're okay?*

What is she threatening? asks the Chilean writer at our now weekly coffee.

I tell her that my mother wants to remind me there is evidence. She could find proof. She could make a case—more than enough documentation of all my various diagnoses, prescriptions, and probations—against my right to be a mother to my children and there would not be shit that I could do.

Would she take them? she says.

Probably not, I say.

I sip my coffee, look down, then up. *I was sick a while*, I say.

What kind of sick? she asks.

Depression, I say. *Anxiety? So many diagnoses*, I say, shaking my head and looking down.

I'm bored already by how pedestrian I find these diagnoses. How I'm just like everyone I know who thinks.

And they'd hold that against you? She looks up from her plate.

They'll hold it over me abstractly. They want me to remember always that they could *hold it against me, while maintaining sufficient plausible deniability that they've done anything wrong.*

I think she'll respond but she doesn't. She catches the eye of the waiter and he comes over. She orders us two gin martinis and we wait for them and are quiet. When they come the glasses sit close together, each with a lemon-rind twist. She nods toward mine and lifts hers and we clink them, quietly, before we take a sip.

THE NEXT DAY, I'm at work and my husband texts me a photo of him holding our girls in our apartment. They're all grinning. The two-year-old has hold of his face with both her hands. I leave early and decide to walk the twelve miles home instead of taking the train. I figure at some point I'll get on the subway, but I don't. I still have that feeling, leaving work now daily long before I'm supposed to, that I'm supposed to be somewhere doing something, but I also think maybe what I have to do right now is walk.

An hour in, I call my mom.

What was that supposed to be? I say.

I just worry, she says. She just worries, but she also likes me afraid.

About what? I say. *If you worry, why don't you talk to me?*

I've been functional for years now, but I think it is a functional that is difficult for them to make sense of. I think they thought when I got better, I'd be better than they think I am.

You don't talk to me, she says.

Okay, Mom, I say.

She starts crying then, and I know I'm supposed to ask her what I can do to help her, to tell her that I'm sorry. I'm supposed to tell her everything is fine.

She's telling me that she just doesn't know why it's not ever enough for me, all her trying, all her loving. My eyes are dry and I know that I will not start crying. I feel fury at her for crying like this, fury at myself for not being willing or able anymore to care.

Mom, please, I say, trying to sound careful. *Mom,* I say. *It's okay. I'm sorry*, I say, accidentally.

I am your mother, she says. Still crying.

I know, I say.

She stays quiet.

I'm sorry, I say. I've said it once and now it seems that I can't stop.

I thought, she says. *I thought when you became a mother . . .* She says the word like it holds something that I have refused to see or understand. That I've got it now, it's been given to me, and that I've ruined what it's meant to mean.

I'M STILL NINETEEN; she's still twenty. I sit alone in my attic room because she left and order chicken fingers and French fries every night and read and watch TV and try hard not to talk to anyone. I sit out on the roof and all the undergrads file out at night to go places I don't know about, have little interest in without her. I hardly go to class, much less have other friends, and I watch them, listen to them talk to and yell at one another. I watch them walk out hopeful, underdressed, and buoyant. I watch them come home hours later, still out on the roof, just watching. They're disheveled, touching one another, in different groups or pairs.

We are very good at desperate emails tinged with self-destruction. Hers are more active, more interactive. We have lives that look concretely, wholly separate, lives that, if one were to track back to the causes, to the feelings and the thinking, might feel largely the same. My depression is the flattest; it's so boring; it's all inward—in books, at least, as well as in her emails, the characters all *do* things. They have too much sex; they drink; they travel and their lives at least are filled with stories that they might tell later when they're older and they're better, when they're the grown-up versions of these unformed, reckless things. I envy her these stories, their shape and texture, the concreteness of her self-destruction. She is looked at, and because she's looked at, she lives her anger and her sadness out loud and people see; I disappear and so slip down and under. I, sporadically, quite violently, try to be seen and am then further knocked down by how completely that effort fails. I ride the T, and I cry and my hands shake and I imagine that someone will notice, will say something, will take me home with them and tell me how to live, but people look afraid or look away or don't notice to begin with. The barista at the coffee shop I used to go to with her seems so horrified by my crying and my shaking hands, even as I order the same quiche and chocolate cake and give him money, that I stop going, just to not have to see what I look like on his face as I hold my hand out for my change.

I don't talk and no one notices that I'm not in class or at the campus center. I buy tubs of Betty Crocker icing at the 7-Eleven that is far enough off campus that I won't accidentally run into one of the four people I know. I get the chicken fingers I subsist on delivered, when I know my roommates are in class or at a party; I try very hard to only go downstairs to pee or shower when they're out. I do not sleep but also do not leave my bed and sometimes, just to prove my ineffectuality more surely, I walk around Boston late at night and nothing happens; I walk back to my attic, take my clothes off, get in bed.

She has three love affairs that year and starts selling weed to friends for cash. Her dealer is in love with her; sometimes they have sex, and she uses the discount to pay for her own stash. She lives off campus with two also-gorgeous girls who have tattoos on their forearms—one of them has her nose and eyebrow pierced—and they drink beer before they eat breakfast and when I go to visit her I feel young and small and far away. I hate her maybe. I want her mostly just to feel as sad as I do, to be as trapped, if only so that she doesn't get too far ahead of me while I'm still the same.

It's cold still. I've lost track of time and do not know the day or month or whether there's some place I'm meant to be or have been meant to be this whole week. It's cold and I'm not wearing enough clothes, running tights, a long-sleeved shirt, no gloves or hat, and I've run out to the Charles River in the middle of the night. I stand on the MIT Bridge, the one, in summer, we walked over every day; the water's frozen at the edges but not in the middle. I have my cell phone with me and I call. *There's something wrong with me,* I tell her. *What is feeling like?* I ask. She's in love again. All she seems to want to talk about is this man she loves, who won't love her back, who sometimes shows up at her house at night and they have sex but does not yet acknowledge she exists in the light of day. She says my name over and over. *Where are you?* she says. *I'm on a bridge,* I say. I don't know then but I know now that we're both children. I want her to feel scared, I know both now and then. I want her to feel more for me than any other person. I don't care the shape it takes: fear, or love, or sadness. I want her close to me. I want her to feel like she can't ever leave. She starts to cry and I tell her to stop it, *There's no need to worry.* I don't mean this. I've called because I want her to cry and I want her to be scared.

I need you to go home, she tells me. *I need you to turn toward your apartment and I'll get in the car and meet you there.* She's hours from me. She says my name again. Her voice, I later learn, is thick with weed as well as all her worry, all her sad and sorry. Then, I think she has so much power, but later I will see all the ways she feels almost completely at the mercy of the wants and needs of other people just like me. I'm so happy that night, though, to have finally found a way to make her come to me.

She talks and cries and I hear her muffled voice and then another person. I hear her start her car, but I stand still. In my memory, she comes to the bridge, but I'm not sure this is what happens. In my memory, she saves me that night; that night I think maybe everything will be okay. It's only the next morning that I see them, out front of our house while she sleeps in my bed and I sit on the roof: my parents, harried, exhausted, rushing out of a cab and coming up our front-porch steps.

Bitch, I say, beneath my breath, as I watch them ring the bell, as I hear her rustle, as I climb in through my window, knowing then that I am absolutely by myself.

Why the fuck, my mother will say later; they will walk me, both of them, to the university offices and tell them I am a danger to myself and must be monitored more closely. The university will balk and want to kick me out, but my parents will not agree to this and my mom will threaten various things, citing statutes that might be made up, and then the university will decree I see a therapist three days a week instead. I will be on probation and they will try sometimes, my parents, they will call and tell me to take care of myself and ask me about class. They will feel both wholly overwhelmed and scared. It will have been years, by then, of me being more than they can handle. They will have tried therapists and so many different medications. They will have tried yelling at me, begging; none of it will work. Sometimes, when my mother is too tired and she gets a bill from the therapist, she will call and yell at me and ask me why I can't just suck it up and be better. *What did we ever do?* she'll ask me. *Why the fuck*, she'll say, *do I have to pay someone to talk to you?*

I'll drive one day in the car with my father, going somewhere, the second time they come up to see me after she has called them, and he will look so revolted by the fact that I am crying. I think now: he must have been so scared. *Stop it*, he'll say, over and over, but I won't stop it. He'll reach his hand up to my face as if he might stop the tears from coming and he will breathe in once, too tired to have hold any longer of whatever patience he might have had before this. He will slap me, once and hard, across the face.

And then Sasha in the background. They've always been nice to her. We're young and she was scared. When she thinks "parent" she thinks a different thing than what they are. She writes me email after email and for a while, I like the feel of not responding. I like her asking, begging, saying that she's sorry, until I can't stand it any longer, not having her to talk to, until she's desperate, until the man she's been courting all semester has fucked one of her roommates and she's begun to disassemble, until we're galvanized, alone again together against every other thing.

4

I SLEEP PAST my first alarm and then my second. At 5:40, my husband reaches for me and asks if I'm going to go run. This annoys me, though I can't say why it annoys me. He tries to pull me to him but I roll closer to the wall, my back toward him, and he climbs out of bed. The coffee grinder whirs and I close my eyes again. At 6:40, which is ten minutes before I am supposed to leave for work, he calls to me from the kitchen. He's making breakfast and packing the children's lunches.

You getting up? he says.

I skip my shower, skip my breakfast.

He pours me coffee in the mug I bring on the subway each day and I hug and kiss both children as they unfurl themselves from their small beds. When I'm halfway down the stairs the two-year-old comes running out of the apartment.

Mommy, she says.

I give her one more hug.

Don't leave.

Josslyn comes out of her apartment and she picks her up.

On the train, I check Sasha's Facebook for an announcement about her baby. I check every other day, mostly knowing it won't change. I'm not friends with her husband on Facebook. We've never met, and when I go to his page it's only his picture and some posts from years ago. It's possible his settings make it so there are all sorts of pictures to which I simply don't have access. The ultrasound or maybe of the baby, newly welcomed, the bump, her perfect cheeks fleshed out.

In a meeting about SAT preparation, I think about setting up a profile just to see whatever I don't have access to. He looks trusting. I could pretend to be from wherever he says he's from. I try to remember what she looked like pregnant the first time. Both my girls were over nine pounds. When I was pregnant, I was so large people pointed at me on the street.

With the four-year-old, the ultrasound tech told me thirty-three weeks in that I did not have enough amniotic fluid. Our OB was out of town, so—on my phone, on the sidewalk on Fifty-ninth Street and Eighth Avenue—I googled what the cause and consequence of this might be.

Could be the baby has no brain or an esophageal malfunction, said the internet. Could be everything is fine. I tried to call my husband but he was working. I scrolled through my phone trying to think who else I might call. Not my mother, not my New York friends, who were still new and had never been pregnant, who all still thought I was sane then. Not Sasha.

Instead, I sat on Eighth Avenue somewhere below Fifty-ninth Street, leaning up against a fire hydrant, massive belly bulging, and I cried. I held the base of my stomach with both my hands and people stared at me and I stared back at them until it started to get dark and I walked home.

———

I mostly walk now. Week after week, I just keep leaving in the afternoon and no one seems to notice I'm not there. I go to the coffee shop and read. Dorothy West, *The Living is Easy*; Gerald Murnane, *The Plains*; Mariama Bâ, *So Long a Letter*; Svetlana Alexievich, *Secondhand Time*. I walk to the bookstore closest to the coffee shop, my favorite bookstore in the city, small with dark wood floors and two well-curated tables, chosen, specially, by the owner, who is a small, curly-haired man who is often behind the counter, who I see sometimes in other parts of the city and I smile at him, though I'm sure that he can never place my face. I linger, flipping through first pages, knowing that I can't afford to buy another novel, that there is no extra twenty dollars in our account. I get books from the library, order used books online for work and charge it to the high school, but then I walk past this shop and find myself inside it, attracted to the thrill of passing the book across the counter. Books are my specific version of consumption; it's the consumption that I walk inside this store to perform. I want to not be someone who says no all the time to every impulse. I want to not make every choice because it is my only choice. This is a stupid, wasteful way to do this, but I do it—the smell inside the store, the people lingering around me—to play briefly at not caring. I pass a book across the counter that I might not ever read: a biography of an artist I love that costs more than twenty dollars, a paperback of translated Scandinavian fiction that I've read bits of for a month. I leave the shop disgusted and embarrassed, stuff the book in my bag, crumple the receipt. I will dispose of it before I get home, evidence of all the ways I am still a spoiled rich kid, as if my husband will not also see the charge on our account and choose to quietly ignore it or to point to it at our monthly tracking of expenses and I will nod, hot-faced, and look down at my lap.

As I walk, I go to neighborhoods I never go to any longer. I have ID cards from all the universities at which I've been an adjunct and, among them, I get into almost every museum in New York for free. I walk through shows in Chelsea, start reading Artforum. I look at massive canvases of black and white, all charcoal, bloodied heads and children hung from trees, close-up photographs of the ocean and the sky, small bits of vastness blown up, made big. I stand a long time in front of paintings I don't wholly understand and try to let them work on me.

Kayla misses two days of school. I go to the office of the counselor with whom she's close to find out if she knows where she's been but I find out the counselor's been transferred to a middle school. She was advocating for devoting more resources to kids with learning disabilities so she's been sent to work under another, less opinionated counselor in an attempt to be retrained.

Are they replacing her? I ask the twenty-three-year-old who was hired to do data entry but is now sitting at the desk where the counselor met with a full caseload of students every day. There are so few places in the building where it's quiet, and this data-entry person appears to have been the first to learn this space was free.

She says: *Probably?*

On the third day, I see on the live attendance tracker that Kayla's at school and I go into the third-floor bathroom and see her shoes under the door of the extra-large handicap accessible stall and I knock and tell her that it's me.

Where were you? I say.

My mom went on a trip with her new boyfriend.

Did you go with her?

It was supposed to be just for the weekend, so I was supposed to watch my brother, but then she didn't get back until last night.

Kayla's little brother is her favorite person, ten years younger; when she talks about him she stops fidgeting and sits up straight.

You guys were alone? I ask her.

I think probably this is something I should tell the counselor except she doesn't work here anymore.

I'm grown enough, she says.

You cook? I say.

My boyfriend brought stuff, she says.

I think about the bruise she showed me and she sees me looking. *It was fine*, she says.

I look at her and shake my head and she smiles at me.

She says: *You miss me?*

Four of my friends come over. They suggested that we go to dinner, but I can't afford to go to dinner, so I invited them to our house and my husband cooks.

We've all been friends for years; we met in grad school; none of them have children; we see each other much less often now. Most of them have money or have partners who make money. One bought a brownstone with her partner's trust fund and spent a year doing it over; another took a year off of work to try to write a book, moving in with her corporate-lawyer boyfriend, spent three months with him abroad. When both my children were born these women were kind and generous in ways that continually shocked me. They brought us dinner, took our trash out. They sat with me in university offices as I pumped milk.

They don't know about the bankruptcy. I worry already

that I exhaust them. There is no fixing the place that we're in, no saying something that might make it better, so I don't tell them, and, often, when they ask me how I am, I just say I'm tired and get quiet.

One of my friends, the one who took the year off—who is lovely, younger than me, quadrilingual, who is planning a wedding and, when she talks about the wedding, turns away from me and addresses the other women in the room in a way that makes me think she doesn't trust that I'd have much to say about dresses or floral arrangements or how she might do her hair—she brings an acquaintance of ours to this dinner, another woman who is very wealthy, whom our quadrilingual friend describes whenever she brings her up as *elegant, just so elegant*. She has some great job in which she works from home a couple hours a day and makes some absurd amount of money because she's smarter than nearly every other person that she works with and they think the work she does should take all day.

This place sounds awful, says this woman I know least well of all the women, speaking of my job.

I nod, then shake my head, not sure what to say.

I keep looking at my friends, wondering if they feel equally annoyed by nearly everything this woman's saying. She also has a baby, the only one besides me, except she has a full-time nanny. Except, she says, she sends her husband to their country cottage with the baby every weekend so that she can *get a break*.

You should leave, this woman says about my job. *It sounds so awful.*

She wears tight, high-waisted jeans and a tucked-in black T-shirt. She has a shock of white-blond hair and she's lined her eyes on top.

I can't leave, I say.

She thinks I mean because I can't leave the students, which is not untrue, but mostly, I can't leave because we wouldn't be able to pay our rent.

This woman sighs this big, long sigh that I think is supposed to be a sort of compliment-slash-show-of-solidarity between us. I know that if I were to sit with her by ourselves and talk a long time I'd probably like her. My quadrilingual friend is kind and brilliant and exacting and I trust she likes this woman because she is too. But I don't have the space to sit and talk with her, to listen to and try to like her, so I sit and I allow myself to hate her, because I'm tired and it's easy. I look at my friends around the table and wonder what they'd do if I stood up and I hit her.

You're a hero, she says.

No I'm not.

Why do you stay, though? asks the Chilean writer a day later; her questions I don't mind because I've decided that I like her. *It can't be only the money.*

I love them, I say. I can't say it without feeling like some bullshit movie that's supposed to make you feel good, some bullshit movie that perpetuates the narrative that black and brown kids need earnest white people to rescue them.

The Chilean writer smirks at me.

I'm good at it, I say.

The kids are smart and, maybe more importantly, they're children. They're teenagers, eager, malleable, and thoughtful. I get to ask them questions, talk to them, I get to make them think. It's thrilling in all the minutes that it's going well and I think maybe, every third or eighteenth minute, that they're learning something. It's thrilling when they listen, thrilling when they argue and they think. It's thrilling, but also, I'm embarrassed by how much I love them, by how little it is they're getting from me, how whatever I give them isn't anywhere close to what they need. I hate every time that someone says how good it is, my teaching these kids, because I'm embarrassed that I thought it might be too at first. That after years of fighting to get to be a college teacher, I was still so often shocked by how little my students needed or even wanted what I had to give. That I came to this school partially because I thought helping would feel good, because I thought I had something to offer, here. That I should have known better, that intellectually, I did. That what my students do need—an obliteration of the same systems I grew up in, a burning down and re-creation of the spaces that I relied on all these years to keep me safe—I can't do and don't know how to.

We go on a field trip to the New York Botanical Garden train show on the Metro-North and we corral the kids onto one train and then another.

Why are we doing this shit? one of my kids asks me as we walk on a wooded, tree-lined path. It's warmer than it's been the past few weeks and sunny.

It's a gorgeous day, I say.

I know, she says.

This lady makes us do this shit because it's for rich white people, says another student.

"This lady" is the CEO of this school where I teach. I shrug and do not talk because I do not think that they are wrong.

We watch a video about the making of the train show.

All I fucking do is ride the train, says one of my students.

When we get inside it's warm and there are plants all around us. The trains are small and made of sticks and twigs and pieces of plants. They're beautiful though strangely alienating. We're a pack of people. My other coteachers are both black women. None of our kids are white. No one else besides our group is black or under fifty and they gawk at us.

What are they doing here? one woman says as she walks past us.

I'm so angry I can't see and almost grab hold of her arm to scold her; one girl turns to another girl, laughing, pointing at me; *Miz is going to hit a bitch*, she says.

On the train ride home, we let the kids get off as we pass close to their apartments, and my coteachers get off farther downtown.

I sit alone another forty minutes to the train I'll have to transfer to to get to Brooklyn. I read Nadine Gordimer, *The Conservationist*. I scroll through Instagram and realize I haven't searched for Sasha there. I pretend she won't notice that I follow her as I follow her, and then I follow him because neither of them is locked and he's right there. I watch a video of a cliff on the coast somewhere in California, then Hawaii. There is a dog, a beach, more cliffs. Pictures of Paris, Vienna, Barcelona. No baby, no bump. Only one picture, the two of them, just their faces, twenty-seven weeks before this; he kisses her cheek, both of them looking toward the camera, smiling, sunglasses on their heads.

At my night class, I teach Magda Szabó's *The Door*, a book about a woman, a writer, and her relationship with her domestic worker. I'm not sure "domestic worker" is the word, nor is "maid." It's her relationship with a woman who cleans her house and cooks for her and her husband, but also, is perhaps her closest, dearest friend. They are not friends, though, because of class; they are not friends because in the domestic worker's moment of desperate need, the main character betrays her violently. This is, at least, how I read the book. There is a moment when the main character could help her friend, her domestic worker, who has no one else, who has loved her intensely over many years, but instead, she calls in strangers, instead, she gives those strangers access to her friend—her friend's greatest nightmare is being vulnerable to strangers—and she drives off in a car to work. I find this book so horrifying, the impact and the power of passivity, the way in which this woman can both love her friend and not ever recognize her humanity, not realize the violence she's enacting, even as she spends days planning how she'll do it, even as she lies about it later on. I cannot breathe when I finish reading. I go into class ecstatic, wore out, scared.

What did you guys think, though? I say after we briefly discuss the book's context.

We discuss the strange space that Hungary inhabited during the Second World War—aligned with Hitler early as well as later occupied, complicit in the crimes committed and later victims of them, yoking themselves tightly with the Allied forces in so many of the later narratives. *In 1949*, I tell my students, *Szabó was awarded one of Hungary's most prestigious literary awards, except the prize was rescinded on the same day*. She'd been named an "enemy of the people" by the Communist Party, which had recently come to power, and would not be allowed to publish for years after that. The book, in fact, opens with the writer character having finally been set free to work again, to be published, the impetus for the hiring of the domestic worker being that she's been allowed to be a writer again after all those years. In a review I read of the novel in preparation, the reviewer says that the book creates the feeling of both being run over by a car and being the driver of the car at the same time. This time, even more than the time before, as I reread, instead of sleeping, every night this week, I felt this in the novel, the specific horror of deep and certain concrete culpability combined with helplessness.

So, I say, *what did you guys think?*

They look at me, wary.

You think it was violent? asks a boy in the back who always talks.

You didn't? I say.

Maybe? he says.

She leaves her, I say. *She could help, and she just goes.*

She sends doctors, they say. *She brings help.*

But she's not there, I say, worked up all of a sudden and cognizant that I should stop this, that this is not the behavior of a grown-up university professor but, maybe, of a frantic, wore-out child.

She doesn't stay, I say. *She says she loves her and she lays her bare for strangers in her most vulnerable state.*

A girl who sits next to me and hardly ever speaks but always takes notes diligently while other students speak, whispers, so I and maybe the three or four people closest to her hear her, she says, *She kills her, basically*.

My husband works on weekends so we don't have to pay for childcare. During the week, while I work, he takes care of our girls. We have an extra thousand dollars in our bank account because he just got paid for a job, so I call the sitter and she comes over and I run fifteen miles and take a thirty-minute shower.

Once the sitter's left, I set up paints on the floor atop a pile of old issues of the *New York Review of Books* and set out paper and old wood from various of my husband's jobs and let the girls make things. The baby nurses and I get light-headed from the running and her eating. They paint the paper and the wood and then their hands and feet and I wonder briefly if I should tell them not to paint their bodies, but it's only watercolors, so then they start painting my face.

I get a news alert on my phone, an hour into painting: a ballistic missile alarm went off in Hawaii, the alert says, but officials say it was a false alarm.

I'm quiet a minute, looking at my phone, then back and forth between paint-covered children.

Can I paint your eyes? the four-year-old says, coming at me with a fine brush covered in purple. I throw the phone up onto the couch, smiling at our daughters. I lie back on the floor with my eyes closed, my hand resting on the baby's calves as she moves around me.

I say: *Only the lids.*

At 2:00 am on Tuesday, the baby starts to cry and I go into her room and her forehead and her cheeks are hot and sweating. When I come back from the bathroom where we keep the baby Motrin, she's thrown up on her sheets. I pick her up and take her clothes off and run a warm bath but she vomits three more times, so I rub her down with a warm cloth, standing her up naked in the bathtub, as she keeps vomiting. She vomits on my clothes too and I take them off and rinse myself and both of us sit in the hallway of the apartment, her hot skin splayed across my legs, in T-shirts but no pants. She's crying off and on and there's nothing left for her to vomit but her fever hasn't broken and I don't want to leave her and she curls up on my lap and falls asleep. At 5:00 am, my husband throws up in the bathroom sink. At 6:00, I email work and tell them that

I'm going to be late. I take the four-year-old to school and my husband's emptied out enough, so he stays with the baby so I don't have to miss the day. At 1:00, the school calls to say the four-year-old has gotten sick, and when I pick her up she's crying and I carry her the mile home because she's too sick to walk and she's vomiting too often to get in a car or ride the train. At home, the baby and my husband are asleep and I wash the four-year-old with another warm cloth and sit with her with an empty plastic mixing bowl until she's also emptied out. I give her tiny sips of water and when my husband and the baby wake up both of their fevers have broken and they go outside for a short walk. I stay with the four-year-old and we watch five hours of *Paw Patrol* and *Dora and Friends* and she falls in and out of sleep. That night, I put everyone to bed and order myself a five-dollar pad thai and sit alone and read.

The next day, I have a fever, but no puking, so I take three Advil, stashing the bottle in my backpack, and I go into work because I only have three remaining sick days and I have to teach my night class anyway. I split my high school students into groups and ask them to close read different parts of the text I assigned the night before and present them, but at my night class, there is no group work, so I lead a three-hour conversation on *Remainder*, by Tom McCarthy, in which the narrator, a suddenly wealthy man without a memory, doubting the solidity of his status as a person, seeks to construct a perfectly controlled representation of what he thinks might be authentic in order to feel real.

During the break, one of my students sees me splashing water on my face and swallowing more Advil and when she asks if I'm okay I hold on hard to the cold sink and nod and smile at her, fever spiking, my head cloudy, and don't say anything.

That weekend, we go to some too-big, close-to-the-water Long Island house in which my husband built two months' rent's worth of walk-in closets.

We get invited to these things after he builds someone a custom closet or redoes their cabinets. The men who own these houses like to open a beer and sit with him as he works on weekends or in the evenings after they come home. They open beers and offer him one; often, he says yes and sticks around.

He went to the same type of college they did, studied the same types of grown-up good-job things. He hated going to the same place every day, had always, secretly, wanted to work with his hands. He'd go after work to a shop he rented and build for hours, just to calm his nerves, to make things, after hours of vagaries. He'd gone to college when no one before him in his family had gone to college and he felt at first that he had to prove something. Once the markets crashed, he had a reason, but also, he had an excuse. He could leave and not just not feel guilty but feel good.

Those greedy fucks, he'd mutter, listening to NPR, as the markets kept tumbling and then the banks were bailed out. He stood close to me—we'd just moved in together—rubbing his thumb along the fresh wear forming on his hands, his suits all dropped at Housing Works, so obviously relieved.

It's a shorter ride on the Long Island Rail Road than my commute to work and we bring the children. My husband's hoping to find his next job. We make small talk, sip too-sweet wine, and he flirts, is charming. I spend long stretches of time sitting fully clothed on the lids of toilets, or searching for or playing with the children, desperate for when he says we can go home.

He's fitter than these other men, a little younger. He's cooler; I never understood the purpose of words like "cool" until I met him. He makes their wives reach up too often to touch their faces or their hair when he is close to them. These men perform for him, say "fuck" too much and unbutton the top buttons of their dress shirts and pick at the labels of their beer bottles and make adolescent jokes.

Their wives linger in adjacent rooms, offering food and calling to the children. I imagine they have better sex the weeks or months he's in their houses, the smell of him lingering in their halls and closets, a monkey wrench or small piece of wood left out.

They are, always, shocked to meet me—my short hair, my mussed-up, too-big clothes. My glasses and the way I use my hands too much when I talk. They look past me sometimes, thinking, maybe, *This can't be right*; they must think: *Her?* She's *a professor*, they mutter to one another, once we start talking, eyebrows raised and smiling, like the word "alleged" sits lodged in the backs of their throats. I nod and redden, try to explain the word "adjunct," which is, perhaps, a cousin of "alleged." I slip, quickly, from making jokes to making everyone uncomfortable. *Except no health insurance*, I say. *Professor*, I say, *of failing to find a way to make a living wage.*

Once, one of the husbands at one of these parties mistook me for the nanny, slipping me a twenty, saying, *Thanks so much for taking such good care of the little ones*. I did not give the money back.

I don't tell them that, as of recently, I also teach high school. I don't know why I don't tell them. I don't want to talk to them about what *good, important* work I'm doing. I think this might be even more demeaning than "alleged adjunct."

They nudge their preadolescent children toward me as if proximity to an Ivy-League adjunct will result, five years from now, in stellar SAT scores. *His teacher says,* they whisper, *that he might be gifted. She loves to write,* they say, *but the teacher resents her spirit, holds her back.* I'm nice to them because I know I have to be and hate them for this, because, if I don't say exactly what I know I should, they might decide they don't want those cabinets or that walk-in closet or whatever other bullshit thing and we might not pay our rent.

I nurse our two-year-old on the couch because I know that they don't like it, would prefer I go to one of the children's rooms *where it's quiet,* where I *have some privacy.* A nice woman comes to me with a blanket; I leave it in a pile on the couch.

I watch my husband, swarmed now by both men and women. I hear him laugh from far away. I see his perfect posture, the easy way he holds his beer, his hand wrapped around the label, his thumb flipped over the lip, the slight stubble on his chin and cheeks. Our girl stares up at me, suckling. Another woman sits next to me on the couch. She's our age, a corporate lawyer. It's always more jarring when they're not older, they're just rich.

You okay? she says. *I'm fine,* I say. I watch our four-year-old flit through the room with a pack of older kids.

They're so beautiful, she says.

I nod.

She places her hand on her stomach and I wonder briefly if she's pregnant.

We've been trying, she says.

I try to decide whether to ask more questions, whether to

lean toward her like I would lean toward her had I not already decided to dislike her, to let her hold the two-year-old once she's done nursing, just to have the memory of the weight of her in all the months until she has one of her own.

She says: *You want some wine?* I shake my head.

She grabs hold of my girl's feet. *Okay,* she says. She looks at me a second time. *Let me know,* she says.

On the train ride home, both girls fall asleep and I start crying.

We're in public, so he's quiet. What I imagine he might be thinking is always worse than the thing he finally says out loud. We watch a drunk man slap his wife as she stumbles off the train.

He runs his fingers through his hair and rubs his hand down his neck and whispers at me. *What the fuck,* he says, *is wrong?*

I don't know, I say. I rub a thumb over our daughters' wrists and refuse to look at him.

He has hold of the handle of the stroller and I watch his knuckles tighten, his arm beneath his shirt get hard.

Those women, I say.

You just listen, he says. *You just smile.*

Don't you hate them? I say. *It's all so . . .*

They're not really what I hate.

I'm just tired, I say.

You're always tired.

I look down at our girls.

It's just work, he says.

I look out the window.

The girls sleep.

When we get home they're still asleep and we slip them somehow into their beds without their waking. My husband pulls me toward him, into the bathroom. He bends me over the cheap black fake-metal shelving unit I bought from Target when I first moved to New York and he enters me slowly, half apologetic, his hands on my shoulders and then on my waist. The top shelf of the shelving unit holds my few beauty products: mascara, witch hazel, lip balm; the glass moisturizer jar—it's too expensive but my mother buys a jar for me once a year, at Christmas—falls, hard and heavy, on my head, but I stay still and don't make any noise.

He leans down to kiss me when he's finished, but I turn my head to grab a piece of toilet paper. I wipe myself and then I find our two-year-old, awake and hungry; she grasps at me, milk leaking from the breast she doesn't drink from, the curve between my chest and stomach wet and sticky. I listen to him take a shower while she eats.

When you leave me, I say—the baby asleep on my chest and my skin still sticky—I say, *you'll find some girl who smiles and wears appropriate things.* (He had to pull my wool cap off my head half an hour into the party.) *She'll be complacent, easy, a little doughy*, I say. *She'll not be terrified of lipstick or that gunk I think I might need to start rubbing underneath my eyes. She'll devote her whole self to you*, I say. *She'll be interesting but never threatening. You'll love her hard and often right up to the point that you're disgusted by the person you've become.*

We lie a long time, awake but not talking. He climbs down from the bed and takes the baby from me, brings her to her bed. I listen as he pours himself a glass of water. He climbs back up, separate from me. I listen as his eyes close and his breathing shifts and he falls asleep.

For our last session of my night class, I take my students out for drinks. This was common when I was a student in this program. It's grad school and all the rules are loose and fluid. Students ply me with drinks and then say the things they have perhaps thought all semester but have not been able to say in class. Four of them have cried at office hours. I'm the least threatening of all of their professors, a bit more mom than not. I want to give them whatever it is they want for me to give them. But then sometimes what they want is not a thing that anyone could give.

My boss got drunk and tried to kiss me, whispers a girl, her words slurring, who writes often about a trauma she experienced the year she turned sixteen. *I had to ride home in a cab with him and take him up to his apartment because I didn't think he'd make it home and then he tried to kiss me and now I'm scared I'll lose my job.*

Do you think I'm dumb? asks a young girl who writes about death and, once, a strange, riveting piece about a slaughterhouse.

Of course not, I say, meaning it.

People think I'm dumb a lot, she says.

She's blond and pretty, sweet-looking.

I never thought that you were dumb.

At some point, the name of the man my former student mentioned months ago comes up. *He shouldn't be a teacher,* says one of my male students.

He's disgusting, says another one.

He tells girls in office hours that he's in an open marriage, says one girl.

He belittles women, says another.

He's fucked up.

I've had two bourbons and am not sure what to say to all of this. No one has so far offered a specific accusation. I'm not sure how to answer. I'm not sure what's allowed.

I'm sorry, I say. *Has anyone said anything to anyone higher up?*

One of the girls, who every class has lined eyes and lined lips and is much smarter than I thought she was when I first met her, says, *Someone tried to report it to the heads of the department but they shut them down.*

What do you mean? I say. *What did they report?*

I'm not sure, she says.

None of them is sure and none of them seems to have knowledge that's firsthand, concrete, conclusive.

I'm sorry, you guys, I say. *This sucks.*

It's revolting, says one of the men who is most vocal. He is older than the others. *This shit should not still be going on.*

I don't call Melissa. I worry that she'll think I'm being unreasonable. I worry that I ask too much, and I don't want to ask for more that she can't give. Instead, I wait two days and then I call a dean I know and trust, who helped me briefly when I was pregnant my last year of grad school and navigating how to keep my health insurance while not being on campus as much. She comes each semester during one of the two fifteen-minute faculty meetings to repeat the same phrases about *university policy*.

You have a duty to report, she tells us each semester. *If you are a witness to or have knowledge of any of the following,* she says, and then she lists them, knowing full well half the room has tuned her out, all the student grievances that we must contact her about.

So provincial, a fifty-something man had whispered to me at one of these meetings a few months ago, as this dean explained that one could not date a student while she was in one's class. This guy scrolled through Facebook on his phone and shook his head as she told us undergrads were always, regardless of the circumstances, off limits.

They're not children, he added, and I sat still, my hands held in my lap.

First, I write this dean an email asking if she has time to meet with me. I tell her I have something I need help with. She gives me a couple of times that work for me to come in or talk on the phone. I skip out of work in the middle of the day to meet with her.

We make small talk. I make an off-handed joke about wanting to start a commune upstate because New York is too expensive, and she shows me a video on her phone of a plain-faced older woman with long, gray hair who built her own house and farm and what seems to be an anticapitalist self-help YouTube empire about the advantages of going off the grid.

So, what's up? the dean asks after she turns off the third video; she turns her phone screen down on her desk. In this last video, the woman spent most of the time in conversation with her cows.

What's going on? she says.

I'm tearing up but both of us ignore this.

I trust you, I say. *I feel like I should say something*, I say. But I have no firsthand knowledge; I have no evidence, no facts.

Okay, she says.

I start with the student in my office. I say the man's name and tell her about my students that last class. I'm embarrassed suddenly as I tell her we'd been drinking, wondering how this might be dealt with later on.

I think they tell me, I say, *because I'm this weird space of I have no power but am still technically in a position of authority. What they're saying,* I say, *there's nothing tangible, and yet . . .*

I try to explain to her that I'm crying partially because I'm scared to be the person who is in here, that also I don't wholly understand why I am crying. That partially it's because of how common and how pedestrian everything I tell her sounds.

What do you mean, common? she says.

The whole place is systemically icky, often, if you are a woman is not a reasonable or rational thing to say to someone. The whole world is, sort of, so who cares. Ickiness and a low-grade, sometimes destabilizing discomfort are not substantive allegations and I, daughter of lawyers, know this, and yet, now that I'm here, I want to say this too.

I don't, I say, *know many women who took many classes with male professors after their first year. There were maybe four male professors we knew we could trust. I know at least three women who slept with the professors whose classes they took. I know one woman got her short story sent to a fancy publication by her married professor after that.*

She looks at me. I've said this all out loud.

This was consensual, I say.

Do you believe that? she says.

No, I say. *But I'm not them.*

It's literature, I say. *Art,* I say. *Sex and beauty are a part of it. Let's get—* I say. *I just wanted you to know the stuff I heard about this guy. I didn't want to not say anything in case there are more things later on.*

I feel awful and ungrateful.

There are some really wonderful professors up here, I say. I name some of them. *This place has done so much for me,* I say.

Can you come back next week? she says.

She has to go and I have to get back to work for an afternoon meeting about nothing.

Sure, I say.

Before I leave, she looks like she might grab hold of my arm but doesn't. *It's okay*, she says. *It's good to cry.*

I wipe my nose with my sleeve and then I'm embarrassed. I nod.

I know, I say. I shake my head and laugh.

At work, my eyes are puffy but no one says a thing about it. I'm done teaching for the day and, briefly, Kayla comes into the empty classroom where I've hidden to work and tells me about her day. A lot of girls don't like her and there've been rumors spread about her, a litany of Facebook posts that she took screenshots of and the assistant principal had to ask the girls to take them down.

Stupid jealous bitches, she says. She picks at her fingers.

It feels worth saying that she's beautiful. Lips and eyes and cheekbones. Perfect, dark-brown skin. She wears a wrap around her hair this day and positions and then repositions it as she talks and looks past me toward the door.

They need to just take care of their own selves, she says.

I nod.

I want to tell her not to endanger herself, to stay steady. I feel completely ill equipped and don't think anger in this instance is an out-of-hand response. But she's been suspended twice this year for fighting and if she's suspended one more time, she'll get kicked out.

You have to take care of yourself, I say.

Two days later I get an email from the office for equality and affirmative action at the university asking if I have time to come in. I google the woman who sent the email and find out she's a lawyer. When I left the dean's office, I had been under the impression that nothing would happen until we spoke again. I email back quickly and give this woman dates and times when I can sneak out of work and come up to see her. *Tomorrow morning, then,* she confirms.

I draft an email to Melissa but don't send it. I don't want to bother her with more of other people's worry. I figure I can always find her afterward.

I think, my whole run, about how to dress for this meeting. I wear all black, pants and long-sleeved shirt, afraid somehow to show any skin. I'm nervous waiting for her to come out of her office when it's time for our meeting. She doesn't come out. Instead, she stays seated at her desk and the receptionist tells me it's my turn to go in.

Do you know why you're here? the woman asks me.

I think so, I say. My hands start shaking.

You okay? she says.

I'm an adjunct, I say. I shouldn't be so scared and want to tell her what I know and I'm relieved somehow that something's being done.

If anyone tries to retaliate against you, she says, *you can file a complaint.*

So, while I'm unemployed and out this paltry salary that keeps us afloat, I will come up here and cry to her and she will write it down.

Do you want to start? she says, after a back-and-forth about my not being under investigation, after my saying I do have some information about behavior that is questionable.

I have specific questions, she says. *But why don't you go first.*

I tell her the same thing I told the dean just days ago. She asks me for names but I won't give them to her. She repeats back to me, *a friend of your student's friend,* and I nod and she types and I feel dumb.

Is that all? she says.

Maybe, then, it's nothing, I think. Maybe, then, I've gotten all this wrong. I think there's not language, much less legal recourse, for what I've just described to her. What is the statute, the law, the bullet point laid out on the university website, for feeling less than, knocked down, not quite in control, all of the time?

I want to tell her the names of all the professors who never looked at me when I walked by them, when I was in a circle of people talking to them, how it felt like there were prerequisites for being heard or read that had nothing to do with what I thought I'd come there to try to do or say or be or learn. How it felt like smart was one thing for the men, obvious and uncomplicated, often self-appointed; the women who were chosen were anointed instead of self-selected, *brilliant,* they were called instead, which felt like it demanded more of the senses, which always seemed to be attributed to girls some of the male professors liked to look at during and after class.

I think of Sasha then and how she would almost certainly have a concrete grievance in this situation. Someone would have *done* something to her. If we were still talking, I could talk on her behalf.

Is there anything else you might want to tell me? asks the lawyer.

I'm confused now. I feel almost impossibly tired.

Did a student report anything more specific to you? she says.

She tells me a story then that I haven't heard: a student overhearing this same professor in his office with another student, hearing sounds that sounded *inappropriate,* watching the student and the professor walk out mussed up.

We were told she reported this to you and you reported it to Melissa, who did not follow up with us.

Melissa, who's been kinder to me than most anyone.

None of that's true, I tell her.

She nods.

It's not. I feel somehow now like I'm accidentally on his side. False allegations is what I'm saying. *Who would say that?* I want to ask. I want to give her something irrefutable, but I don't have anything like that.

But the other stuff, I say.

She names the student who supposedly told me this story.

I don't know her, I say.

Melissa's wonderful, I tell her. It's an adjective that means nothing, least of all to lawyers. *She's one of the most supportive people, especially to women, in this whole place,* I say.

All right, says the lawyer.

She's stopped writing down any of what I say.

I don't go back to work. I miss a meeting, but I text my co-homeroom teachers; I ask them to tell my boss that there's an issue with my kids. I text the babysitter and tell her that I will get the kids from school and I get on the train and pick them up. They're surprised to see me and they smile at me and I pick them up and it feels like the first time I've breathed in days. I take them to the park and they play and I watch them and then I take them home and we have dinner and I bathe them and I put them to bed.

I call Melissa. I tell her about my conversation with the lawyer.

I think somehow, I say, *you've been accused of something?*

She's quiet a long time.

I just wanted you to know, I say. *None of what she said is true,* I tell her, about the lawyer.

I know, she says. *Thanks for telling me.*

We talk a long time without either of us saying anything substantive. She tells me about her classes, her dog's second round of chemo. We talk as if, if we keep talking, some of what we've both just learned will make more sense, but it does not.

I hear my phone buzz and beep around 2:30. I remember that those stupid Instagram stories track who watches when you watch them. I know before I know that Sasha's found me out.

I don't know how to do this, her text says. *Tell me I won't do it wrong.*

Our two-year-old is sleeping with us, curled up in a ball against my stomach, hot-skinned, breath thick with phlegm from her never-ending late-spring cold. I pull her closer to me and I hold my phone, staring at the screen with her name up at the top, then back down at the baby's hands that she has wrapped around my other wrist.

WHY DON'T YOU *call her?* asks the Chilean writer. I've left work already and we sit and split a large plate of eggs and vegetables and French fries at a small, large-windowed restaurant on West Tenth Street in the middle of the day.

We don't talk, I say.

The only other patron in the restaurant is an old woman with long, thick hair wearing all black.

I say: *So much time has passed.*

The Chilean writer's shoulders hunch and her shirt dips in the middle. She has a mole on her right clavicle; her bones are long and thin.

I can't look at her. *For a long time I thought she'd be the person who would somehow make me be okay,* I say.

The Chilean writer nods, as if we are all, at some point, this deluded.

I was only good at needing from her, I say. *When she needed me, I failed.*

The Chilean writer stays very quiet, stirs some milk into her coffee.

She lost a baby, I say. *Years ago. We were still children.*

I can feel her face get closer to me.

I left her, I say.

It sounds less violent than I feel it. The Chilean writer sips her coffee and looks past me toward the door.

More than once, I say. I say it louder than I meant to and she faces me again.

There is no Big Awful Crime I've hidden. I want to hold the Chilean writer's face tight in my hands and make sure that she knows that sometimes violences are small and subtle, but that only makes them harder to make sense of, to figure out how they might be forgiven, how one might make amends for them later on.

At every moment that she might have needed me to be there, I say, *I shut down and disappeared.*

I'M TWENTY-TWO AND Sasha's twenty-three. I live in New York and don't want, anymore, to be in grad school; grad school seems meant to last a thousand years, and all we talk about is how precarious our lives will still be once we're done. I sleep with a Victorian literature scholar who asks to hold his hands around my neck while we have sex. I let him because I feel I should be grateful to him for wanting to fuck me. He's only the third person that I've slept with, none of them having stuck around more than a few days or weeks.

She has an extra room in her apartment in Taipei, where she's gone to learn Mandarin and teach English and *have an adventure,* because the prestigious fellowship to which she applied did not let her in. She says *Come* and I have the security deposit from my apartment and want so much to be with her. I think, secretly, that if I go to her, that she'll make everything okay. I get approval for a semester free of coursework and of teaching, in exchange for not taking a stipend. I imagine that our talking can make everything better, like it used to, that being close to her, watching her live, somehow will teach me how to be as well.

She gets stoned every morning and again at night and we watch *The West Wing* over and over; when we watch the episode in which there is a crisis between Taiwan and China, it feels as if the threat is real. My mom is shipping me the Wellbutrin that I've been prescribed but I don't take it; I've never taken it. I can't say why except to say it feels like an assertion somehow of control. Sasha cooks large, indulgent meals after her last joint of the day and is desperate that I join. She buys cheap bottles of wine, and I sip my single glass and she downs the rest.

It's so hot. We think we know hot, coming from Florida, but there's no breeze from the ocean and all the concrete mixed with all the smog, the air's not just hot but thick and every time we go outside we're wet with sweat within blocks. She takes her clothes off as soon as she gets home from work, peeling shirt, then pants, and walks around the apartment in her bra and underwear, gesturing and talking, pulling her hair up off her neck. I sit, fully clothed, on the couch and I stay quiet. She wants, she says, over and over—sex, love, a feeling so intense that it jolts her out of the stasis and the strangeness of our lives in this place; I sit quiet in the corner, wondering why, but also knowing, I can't be that for her. She misses that specific brand of power that comes from male attention—in Taipei, with her height, her brashness, and her volume, men don't look at her like they did at home. What she wants, what she misses, is being wanted, which is a thing I've never wholly had a hold of. I'm relieved at first, that we're alike like that here.

I read Anita Brookner on my mattress on the floor in my small room with the less-well-working air conditioner. I read Jean Rhys, D. H. Lawrence, Colm Tóibín, Deborah Eisenberg, Iris Murdoch, Barbara Comyns, Penelope Fitzgerald, Doris Lessing, Jane Bowles, more Faulkner and Woolf. I like the tighter, sharper, domestic stories; I prefer Fitzgerald's *The Bookshop* to her more famous *The Blue Flower*, Tóibín's *Nora Webster* breaks my heart. I carry pieces of the Eisenberg stories in my head and play them over and over as I ride the subway, as everyone around me says words that I don't understand, *because the time something was happening, of course, you didn't know what it was like . . . It really wasn't* like *anything—it was just whatever it was, and there was never a place in your mind the right size and shape to put it. But afterwards, the thing fit exactly into your memory as if there had always been a place—just right, just waiting for it.* Taiwan feels like this: *Southeast Asia.* My friend Leah keeps emailing asking how I'm doing in Thailand. Sasha and I have jobs teaching wealthy Taiwanese kids whose parents all have homes in the US. We make more money than I have any need for. Our rent and food is cheap and I keep piles of Taiwan dollars in a box next to my bed. All her friends are other expats teaching English. I mostly only talk to her.

We split a joint and walk out to the night market, where we tong leafy greens and meats into plastic bags and hand them to a man to whom she speaks in stumbling Mandarin. He boils all our food inside a pot, then tongs it back, still steaming, into our plastic bags. We walk, slurping our wet, hot food with chopsticks, and watch a tall, thin man charm a large black snake, beading eyes and shimmering skin; another has itself wrapped around his neck as he works. We pass booths of textiles, meats, and toys and buy loose-fitting linen skirts. One night, we go through a single purple curtain and she cheers and smiles and holds my hand as a small, stout woman pokes a needle through my eyebrow skin. I hold her hand as she gets the cartilage on top of each of her ears poked and filled with small studs and we get shaved ice with sweet fruit juice over the top. All around us words fly out but I can't understand them. I like not having to parse their meaning; they add texture, engulf our daily life, but I'm not expected to respond. After our piercings and our shaved ice, she buys a third bottle of wine from a twenty-four-hour convenience store and we sit in a park late at night and talk and talk; I think this is exactly why I came. I like that no one looks at either of us. I'm so very relieved.

But she's drunk all the time. She's stoned from early in the morning, goes out with friends I don't like. I stay in my room when they come over. They bring ketamine, Vicodin, and cocaine, other drugs that I don't hear the names of, that I don't stick around to see up close. I've had eleven different drugs prescribed to me by now and hated all of them. I've spent so much of the last ten years feeling out of control. I slip away with the large bag of bing cherries I've picked up at the fruit stand that day and curl up on my mattress on the floor and read.

I start running again in Taipei. I've run off and on since high school, but always dipping back into stretches of not leaving my apartment, never feeling strong the way it used to make me feel. But here, sometimes, the apartment's too oppressive and I get lost for hours in the back alleys of the city, not knowing the language, not reading the street signs, but still somehow finding my way back. She writes our address in Mandarin on a business card and I carry it with me each time I go running. It gets sweaty in my shorts pocket and the writing bleeds, but I don't ask her for a fresh one. I carry keys and cash and go for hours to be free of her talking and the air is hot and thick and the smog is visible in some places, but I do loops around the small park by our house and sprint through markets, people giving foot massages on the sidewalks. Sometimes old women sitting outside their small fruit stands cheer and I smile and take off.

The night she brings home a one night stand whose last name we'll never learn, I'm in bed like that with my cherries and my book. *Hotel du Lac*: Edith banished to a hotel, *on probation*, after an aborted marriage. I wake up, a cherry pit stuck to my cheek, when they come in. I try not to listen as they stumble to her room. That morning, when I get up to go to work, her door is open and I see them; all day, instructing wealthy six- and seven-year-olds in simple grammar, I have an image of her on top of him, her bare chest and his.

It's a weeknight, a little more than a month later, when she comes home with the first pregnancy test. I think at first that she is joking. I think, briefly, of that time she was twenty and I was nineteen. I wait, another bag of cherries on my lap, *The West Wing* still playing on the TV, still sweaty from my evening run, as she goes into the bathroom the first time. We walk back and forth from our apartment to the fluorescently lit convenience store a block away to buy more tests to double-check. I cut up mango, share my cherries, sit quietly on the couch as she goes back to check again.

We go to a doctor in Taipei and he asks us (he asks her, because I don't speak the language) why we're wasting his time; she will abort the baby, he tells us. Why are we there asking about prenatal vitamins and care? I'm not sure he's wrong but don't say this to her. In all the years since then, I've still never been sure why she decided to keep her. I can say that both of us had come to feel completely sapped of power. We were bored and anxious. Six years later, in that coffee shop, when I stared at the word "pregnant" and thought about my baby, I thought of her, of that angry, dismissive man. I think maybe she wanted someone to love and to love her. When I first think of her as a mother that night—so much of our friendship up until then had been her instructing, guiding, while I listened—I think, *Of course*.

We have a trip planned. For months now, we've been plotting our departure, two months across the region with all the money that we've saved, then heading home. We've pored over maps and scheduled planes and trains and buses. Our jobs have ended. She's shocked but still we empty our apartment, sell most of our things and leave the rest for our landlord. We pack backpacks and take a flight from Taipei to Vietnam. The plane is small and smells of cigarettes and stale, cold air and she vomits off and on the whole time. She vomits on a bus to Sapa, at a night market in Ho Chi Minh City, in alleys, hostel bathrooms, restaurant napkins. She fights with a pedicab driver in Hanoi, who takes us for a two-hour ride outside the city that we haven't asked for. By the time he lets us out—still far from our hostel, late at night, and lost—she's screaming at him and he's refusing to let go of her arm. She's frantic and she's angry, but I think then that knowing how to fight might be one of the most important parts of what's about to happen to her, and I feel briefly less afraid.

That night, I take her luggage and mine and leave her at an internet café. I go into what looks like the fanciest hotel within walking distance and put a night on my (parents') credit card. I've been without my parents' money a couple of years already, living off my stipends and waiting tables three nights a week in New York, but they sent me a credit card before I left. I'll cut it up soon after this. But this night, I buy her tonic water (the only thing that she can keep down) and Western potato chips and, once I've brought her to the hotel, I run her a warm bath. We watch TV and sit up in the warm, soft bed together and for one of the first times maybe since I met her, we don't talk at all.

When she decides, a few days later, in a hostel in Cambodia, to go home, she expects me to go with her. We call her sister, who, whatever I think or say about her over all these years, is there for her, both before and after, in ways that I am not. We start to plan. The whole time we talk as if I'll come with her. Right before we call the airline, though, I realize that I won't. This is maybe more agency than I've ever had in front of her, perhaps the first time I've chosen to be separate from her since we met. I can't fathom right up to the point when I say so that I might choose it. I feel both scared and impossibly relieved once I do.

We're in a hostel phone booth in Phnom Penh as I tell her I'm not going with her and she sits and I stand and watch her fingers clutch the old, black phone and I watch pedicabs fly past her out the window, hoping maybe I'll just disappear.

I'm going to stay, I think, I say.

I can see her shoulders still, her flat, scared face. I feel emptied out and free all of a sudden. For weeks I've been trying to help her, somehow fix this or make it better. All this time I wanted her to need me, but I can't give to her whatever she needs now. I sit with her as she calls the airline. She's spent more money than me. For weeks before we left, I doled out more and more of the cash I kept by my bed, and we kept a tally on the fridge of what she owed. She spent so much more on weed and evenings out, and I paid most of our rent.

I'll pay you back, she says, as I hand her my parents' credit card so she can give the number to the airline.

It's not my money, I say.

I'll pay them back, she says.

The day after she leaves I spend walking through an old school close to the killing fields outside Phnom Penh, now turned into a makeshift memorial: classroom after classroom, I stare at rows of murdered faces. Different rooms contain different sexes: board after board of men and boys; row after row of women and girls. Days later, I'm in Siem Reap and wake up before the sunrise. I've hired a young guy to drive me around Angkor Wat and we watch the sunrise through the main temple and I forget to take a picture, shocked still, each time I turn, that she's not there.

I imagine all those hours of her flying, nauseous still, I'm certain. I want to go to her, follow her home, if only briefly. I track the hours I know have had to pass to get her off the plane and somewhere safe and settled. Her sister's there to meet her. They email from a hotel in Miami and I'm relieved that she's in someone else's care.

I stay five more weeks and we write long emails back and forth the whole time. It is, in some ways, the best our relationship has been in months or years. From hostel hallways and internet cafes, in Thailand, Laos, Cambodia, so alone that I go days or weeks hardly talking to other people, I can pour myself out loving her, knowing she will take in all of it, knowing she's so many thousands of miles away and cannot come to ask for more. My whole life, I'll be better at this type of friendship and feel guilty for it; I like being needed, giving, but not so close that I can't run away.

A month later, in Florida, both of us are back with our parents while I wait for school to start. She calls, she texts almost every day. Her body's changing but not enough that anyone but I and her family can see the difference. She's tired and she's sick but it's not clear what of her nausea is hormones and what's being afraid. We go for the same long walks on the beach we used to take in high school. We talk and talk except the tenor's different. Everything feels heavy, everything is shaped and weighted differently by what lies ahead.

She goes out to California. She does not want to be the knocked-up girl in our small Florida town and though it smells a little like it was not wholly her choice, I understand why she wants not to know anyone in the place where she'll become a mom. I am not privy to her conversations with her mother. She's known me almost half my life but I'm not comfortable at their house anymore, afraid somehow that her mother finds me culpable. I imagine her mother wants her to have the baby somewhere where people won't assume this is an aberrance, like her beauty and her brilliance, that her mom passed along.

Her mother's brother takes her in. She has a room overlooking their pool up in the hills outside LA where she reads and studies for her MCATs and waits for the baby. She says she wants peace and time to think, none of the people we grew up with asking how she's doing, wondering out loud about the father; she doesn't want her mother every day pretending this is all just exactly as she'd planned it all along. Sometimes, when she calls to tell me about what it feels like, the sound of her on the machine at the doctor's office, where she goes by herself, the pictures that she texts of blacks and grays and whites that look like shadowy mush, I try to picture her as Mother, and it makes a certain kind of sense. It's so concrete. She'll have someone to love always, something sure to be.

She says she'll come back east and we can raise the girl together. I don't ever quite acknowledge this because I think it's just a thing she says to include me. I assume, when she's there in front of her, she'll go home to her mom. I'm back in grad school and she says she'll find a job close by, apply to med school. The mystery of it, and the magic, has awoken something in her and, once again, I have flashes of feeling, somehow, that she's found her way to a world I can't quite touch.

They won't know what happened when it happens. She'll go in for one of the thousand checkups one has to go to in the final trimester, thirty-eight and one half weeks. They'll attach her to the machine that checks the baby's heart and there won't be a sound and the doctor's face will get stiff and her nose will wrinkle and she'll fiddle briefly, almost calmly, with the machine. There will be quiet where there should not be quiet and she will sit and she will wait.

We have to . . . the doctor will say.

She'll bring a nurse in.

Is there someone you could call?

Her uncle shows up, silent, after she calls her mother, who cannot get on a plane until the next day with her sister.

Three days later they'll induce her. I won't be there. The labor will stall and they'll have to cut her from her. More silence then, the shivering from the anesthesia, epidural; her teeth will chatter and they'll pull the curtain just below her chest as they remove her. I'll have the same thing happen, six years later, except when my baby comes we'll hear her and we'll hold her; I'll make my husband open up his shirt so she can settle in against his chest as they stitch me back up—when hers comes out, the whole room will stay still.

I go to her three weeks after, once her sister's gone back east to school, her mom's flown home. She's a blank, soft space, stiller somehow than I've ever seen her. I crawl into her bed with her the night I get there; every night I'm there I lie close to her and

I'm not sure either of us sleeps but we lie quiet, bodies warm. It's our first glimpse of death up close, but also, it's our first glimpse of birth. We swim every morning in the pool below the room where she still stays in the house that seems always to be empty. We float and I try hard not to look for signs of her beneath her one piece. We walk to the farmer's market close to the house and I try to make her dinner. I'm an awful cook but we get vegetables and fresh eggs and cheese and I make us large salads with store-bought dressing in paper bowls and we set them on our laps, the TV on most of the time, movies and shows we watched when we were teenagers. We walk and walk, we swim and eat, but hardly talk. The third night I'm there, I sit in her bed reading and she's a long time in the shower and, every time she's in the shower, I think I hear her cry. When she comes out, she has one towel around her hair and one held up at her chest and she stands in front of the full-length mirror in the room we sleep in. She wears underwear but nothing else and points to the still-smarting scar beneath her belly; it's so low she has to hold her underwear down with her thumb to show me, and she pulls my hand over the length of it, rough and bright red, jagged. *It's proof*, she tells me, eyes splotched red and swollen. *That she was there.*

Nine days after I get there—because I don't know what to say and I can't help her, because she's signed up for more classes and I tell myself that she'll survive it; because all there is is empty space that I can't fill—I hug her and I hold her and I make her promise that she'll text me every day and tell me if and when she needs me; I'll come back whenever. I fly back to restart school.

I don't know why she doesn't go home to Florida. Her uncle's gone for work most of the time and she's in that big, quiet house all by herself. It will be two days after I leave her alone in California before she calls a dealer, a guy we both know from high school who lives an hour away. He'll sell her weed and pills and she'll come back the next week. She'll have just signed up for an MCAT course and claim the drugs steady her. She will have gotten Vicodin and Oxycodone to *take as needed, whenever the pain gets to be too much*, after the C-section. She'll be told, just as I am later, to take it on a schedule, *to get ahead of the pain*.

I will text her, daily at first and then weekly. I will ask her how she is, but there will only be so many ways to say that she is fine, that she has no job or friends but she's still there. It will be almost a month after I leave before we talk on the phone again. It's the fact of trying to fill up all that silence, mostly, that keeps me from picking up the phone. She's cooking most of her meals and swimming in the pool we swam in; she's still waiting for her life to start.

She'll ace her MCATs. When she gets into nearly every med school she applies to, I'll see her mother post about it on the internet and I'll send her a text saying *Congrats* and she will text back *Thanks*.

A long stretch of time will pass then in her absence. It will pass for her, and for me, but not ever together. I'll talk about her sometimes, *my oldest, dearest friend*, I'll say, and then I'll turn red and have to go splash water on my face.

I'll get married and she'll come—she'll be in the wedding—and it will feel strange how little she knows or even seems to want to know the man that I am marrying. She will sit next to me as I get my hair done—paid for by my mother—talking to me, just like always, thinner than I've ever seen her, her feet up on the hairdresser's supply kit, her own hair loose and wild down her back. She'll tell the woman, who twists my hair at the base of my neck, what best suits me. She'll stand next to her at one point, loosening dark strands around my face. She'll bring a man whom I remember only as pale and tall and, once, as I am walking among the different tables greeting people, as I've been told it is my job to be greeting people, I'll see his hand slipped high up underneath her dress and watch her face stay flat and passive as he grins and the thin fabric of her skirt rises slowly up and falls again.

Years will pass then. She'll become more frantic as I start to feel more steady. We won't know how to be with each other without her there to guide us both. We'll talk sometimes once a week and sometimes once a month. There will be gaping holes of space of missed calls and unreturned text messages, both from her to me and me to her; there will be hours—when I do pick up and she's sad or angry; when she has met someone and it hasn't gone well; when no one, nothing, is the thing she wants; when she needs to cry and rage—that I walk around our apartment with the phone pressed against my ear and try to think how else to say the same useless phrases that I'm saying, as my husband motions to me to just get off the phone because dinner's ready, we have people that we're meeting, I have more to read or write or grade and he hates the way I look emptied out right after, because he's heard me say the same thing in different forms for hours now, then years.

We're dressed to go to dinner with a client of my husband's who's suggested maybe he'd be interested in opening a furniture store. It's two years after he quit his job and one of the first of all the many times we wonder if our choices were all wrong. We're walking to the subway and she calls me and I answer. I won't go down the stairs until she isn't crying anymore.

What's wrong with me, though? she says.

Nothing, I say, and I mean it. *You're my favorite person in the world.*

She's been broken up with. She's aced every year of med school and has her pick of residencies across the country, but she still wants most of all, maybe just like everybody else, to feel safe and loved. Her mother and her sister are exhausted by her. They have patience for her for the first little while, but they, like me, get worn out.

It's cold out and my husband makes a show of pulling up the collar of his coat.

I'm just tired, she says.

I know, S.

I don't want to have to try at this again.

We hear two trains come and go and she's still talking. My husband says my name so she can hear.

What's his deal? she says, angry.

Sash, I say. *We have to . . .*

She cries harder and I put my hand over the phone.

Just go, I say. *I'll meet you.*

My husband mutters something I'm glad I don't hear, looks at me pleadingly one more time, and heads down the subway stairs alone.

A phone call I don't answer and then don't return because I am, I tell myself, exhausted, qualifying exams and building a dissertation. I send pithy text messages telling her I'm thinking of her, which, sometimes, I am. I miss her, desperately; I know no one like her. The people I know in New York all know me only as a grown-up; we're polite and functional, make plans weeks in advance. Sometimes I think of her and want only to be with her. But then either I get her on the phone or just linger long enough on the thought of her to remember the her I miss is not the one I'd get if I called. Messages I listen to at first and sometimes, at first, respond to, then her name, on my voicemail, after a preliminary dissertation conference: her name with the blue dot next to it that means the voicemail has not yet been played, a deep breath in, closing the phone, the blue dot haunting me for days, then months. Whole years pass. And then just swiping right and tapping, watching as I disappear them, exhausted by the prospect of her needs that day; not talking to my husband that week, back in therapy because he cannot fix me and I am angry at him for not helping to fix me. Back in therapy because grad school health insurance might be the last good health insurance of my life. *Boundaries are an okay thing,* says the therapist when I talk about Sasha. *But she needs me,* I say. I'm pregnant, and he motions toward my stomach. I am partially in therapy because everyone's afraid for me. *Postpartum depression is a real concern,* they tell me. *Get rest, and focus on the baby,* they say. I am not yet done with graduate school and also tending bar for extra money. *She is not a child,* says the therapist, about Sasha, as I hold my hand under my belly. *You have plenty on your plate.*

One year later, as I nurse our five-month-old around the clock while trying to write my dissertation, Sasha will eat a bottle of Oxycontin alone in her apartment close to the hospital where she's chief resident, and she will have to take a leave of absence and her mother and her sister will fly out to be with her and she'll send me a letter, asking me to come get her from the rehab where they sent her that she hates. She will not call me, not during and not after. I'll write her back something dumb about how much I love her, but that I think that she should listen to her sister and her mother. I don't love her. I don't know what love is, she'll say, in the letter filled with fury she sends back to me. *What in the fuck*, she'll ask me, *have you ever done for anyone but read and speak and think?*

THE CHILEAN WRITER eats a spoonful of the crème brûlée we've somehow ordered. I've talked and talked and now want mostly to be quiet. I hold my coffee with both hands.

You were so young, she says.

She was also, I say.

What could you have done? she says.

It's a question that I've heard before and hate and want no part of.

Shown up.

And now? she says.

We're grown-ups, I say; *we text. I stalk her on the internet once my children are in bed.*

And she's pregnant? she says. *She's better?*

I don't know what that means, I say.

5

My husband's taken a job out of town for three weeks and I have to go in late to work while he's gone. I keep asking for concessions. I keep sloughing off responsibilities on my co–homeroom teachers—kids I ask them to check in with, readings I want to make sure my students get for which I do not trust the twenty-four-year-old—and only think enough to feel guilty about it afterward.

I'm pretty sure by now I won't get fired no matter what I ask for. I'm a thirty-four-year-old J. Crew–cardigan-clad white woman with an Ivy-League PhD, and, though both of my co–homeroom teachers work harder than I do and are better at their jobs than I am, when the CEO walks from classroom to classroom to watch all of us teaching, she always reports back to the principal that she likes *the feel* of me.

I take both girls to school and it feels magic to get to do this daily. They fight with me sometimes and sometimes with each other and they cry and do not want those socks or that dress or that underwear and sometimes they lie on the floor by the front door and scream because the seams on their shirt are rubbing wrongly on their collarbone again. But still, I get to hold their hands and walk them to the bus and ride it with them. I walk them each into their classrooms, and I linger, knowing that I'll be late, as they sprint up to their friends. Sometimes, they sprint back, to kiss me on the leg, ask for one more hug. I put them in the running stroller early and I run them a loop around the park before school starts, packing my clothes and bag into the bottom of the stroller, changing in the school bathroom, locking the stroller up close to the school and going into work still smelling of sweat.

I'm scrolling through Sasha's Instagram a week before my husband gets back: more vacations, coastal pictures. She went to see her sister. Her mother visits. I can only see above her chest in all the pictures; I wonder, though, if she was pregnant after all. I count the weeks between each photo, try to match them with the texts she's sent. I imagine her close to due now, showing, surely. I reconsider making up a profile to befriend her spouse on Facebook.

We haven't been outside all day and the girls are getting antsy, but also upset at the prospect of having to put on coats and shoes. I convince them, finally, getting a text from my husband asking what we're up to and wanting to say, truthfully, that we've been outside. The elevator takes too long and we climb down the stairs, both girls with a toy and book, still fighting over who got what and why. We pass a man standing on the landing and they stop crying to wave and smile at him and I laugh, remembering how quickly they can switch.

That night, I'm back looking at Sasha, the computer whirring too close to my face, and I hear something outside our door explode. I jump up to wake the children, who have been asleep for hours after the afternoon spent in the park.

I smell the smoke. The fire alarm.

Sprinklers run and the air is filled with smoke. I hold both girls to my chest and carry them quickly down the stairs, phone and keys and wallet in my hand and their blankets wrapped around their backs.

What's going on? the four-year-old asks me.

Her sister is wide-eyed, the two of them looking at me, then one another, their cheeks still hot and red with sleep.

I don't know, I say. *It's fine.*

The two-year-old cries off and on and asks for her father. *Daddy, Daddy,* she says, delirious still with sleep.

Everyone's outside—so many of us, but we're never together all at once. Our building is half rent-controlled and half gentrifiers who can't afford renovated apartments. It's old and brown and black and young and white and the groups all clump together. I look around for the handful of neighbors I know from the elevator, start searching for Josslyn.

The firemen come to check us and I ask them if they've seen her.

6C, I say to no one. *Check* 6C.

It's cold and they bring a city bus to store us. Many of the tenants are old and need their medications. Many of us aren't wearing coats. The cops bring us rough dark-blue wool blankets that I cover myself and our girls in as the bus runs and I hold them and stare at all the neighbors whose names I do not know but whom I have smiled at for years. Seven floors, each with four apartments. Some of the apartments hold two or three families.

Another woman, a newer tenant, also a young, white mother, leaves her husband to come ask if we're okay.

I want to call my husband but am not sure what to tell him,

not sure what has happened. I don't want to scare him, make him feel worse for having to leave us to go work.

I go up to the Dominican man who gave my husband cigars the week after both girls were born with a card that said *Congratulations*, a single flower from the bodega across the street for me. We've mumbled at one another over the years, held the door open. I ask if he knows where Josslyn is. He speaks only Spanish, and I look to the older woman standing next to him and ask her if she knows Josslyn.

No se, they both say, shaking their heads at the crowded bus, as people stand, talk, sleep. The girls don't sleep but are quiet, eyes wide open. They wear mismatched pajamas; the two-year-old has hearts on her pants and Santa on her long-sleeved shirt. The four-year-old has trucks and bunnies.

We watch out the window as the firemen file out, then back into the building. The smoke comes from the sixth floor, our floor. I finally call my husband once the girls are back asleep. He asks if I want him to come home, but if he doesn't stay we won't be able to pay this month's rent; we're trying to save enough so that I don't have to teach at the high school in the fall. I tell him it's fine, I'm fine, that he has to stay. That whatever has just happened, there isn't any way that he can help.

A police officer comes onto the bus and says he needs us to account for one another. Another officer comes on and repeats, I think, what the first said in Spanish, then in Mandarin. We go floor by floor. Slowly, everyone on one and two and three and four and five is counted, relief slowly seeping through the bus; *Fine, we're fine*, we all say. When they get to us, the Dominican man and I stand up. The older couple that lives next to Josslyn is not on the bus and the Dominican man calls out for them. The Spanish-speaking police officer stops him, asks him a question. She speaks to her partner, who looks down at a list.

They were sent to a hospital, he says. *Smoke inhalation.*

Josslyn, I say, *Josslyn isn't here,* I say.

I don't know her last name. Six years, and I don't know her last name.

6C, I say. *Have you been in 6C?*

The girls stare up at me with that wired, crazy look of far past tired, far past going to ever sleep tonight.

Sixty-something woman? Black? the cop says.

I walk toward him. *Yes,* I say. *Where is she?*

Ma'am, can you come with me? he says.

The Dominican man is behind him, asking the police-woman in Spanish, as frantic as I am. I grab the girls. They lead us off the bus.

Did Josslyn live alone? the cop asks me.

Someone's found an iPad on the bus for the girls and they watch Dora. Someone's found a bag of Cheetos for them and they sit entranced, orange powder covering their faces and hands.

I think so, I say. *Where is she?*

I run my hands up and down the girls' arms and legs. It's cold out and they don't have sufficient clothes on. The big, rough blanket sits awkwardly around the three of us.

Is she okay? I say.

The cop looks at me, then smiles at the girls without responding.

Would you be able to identify a photograph? he says.

The female Spanish-speaking cop is talking to our neighbor and he grabs my arm as they lead us to a cop car. I grab hold of his hand.

They show us a blurry black-and-white photo of Josslyn. It looks paused, a screenshot. I nod, crying, though I can't say why I'm crying.

Our neighbor keeps a hand around my arm. He goes three times a week to get dialysis. His skin is sallow.

The female cop is speaking to him about the photograph.

Where is she? I ask the male cop.

Did she have children? he says. *A boyfriend?*

She has three kids, I say. She talks about them to me. I know they're grown up but she talks about them as if they're as small as mine.

He shows me another picture. Another screenshot. The man is on the landing between the fifth and sixth floors. He wears a tank on his back.

I get queasy. *He was there today,* I say. I walked by him.

He was standing on the landing and I'd smiled at him. The girls had stopped fighting to smile at him. He'd kept his eyes angled toward the floor.

They nod toward me. Another screenshot, my back, hunched over, both girls holding my hands, their books and toys clutched in their free hands.

That's you? the woman says. I don't realize at first that it's a question. Obviously it's me. I look at them. They've frozen the screen. The girls are looking at the man, his head still down.

I nod.

Had you seen him before?

I look back at our neighbor, who is staring, shocked, at the screen before us, his face even more sallow.

I don't think so, I say. *I'm not sure.*

On the security camera, which I watch, hours later, in the interrogation room with the overly apologetic cops, I see the man in the exterminator's uniform. The girls are in another room with a female cop, more junk food, the same iPad. On the screen, I smile at the man, my lips move. I must have mumbled something. *Hi, hello, good afternoon*, trying to be polite, but my mumbling often isn't loud enough and goes unheard.

He smiled back at me, can slung over his shoulder, the wand for spraying in his hand. *So that's*— I say. He pushed her into the elevator and she stood there, mouth agape, talking, maybe. She screamed or talked or begged. The wand popped up, although he was out of the camera's line of vision. The wand waved past the screen three times and it feels certain in this moment that she's screaming. He threw something small and round in the elevator, the wand disappeared, door slid shut, the screen went black.

They caught him within hours of the explosion. They have him on tape. There were burn marks on his fingers and his face.

I confirm the time they already have on the bottom of the camera screen. I confirm I saw the man, that he was standing in the stairwell.

Had you seen him before? they ask over and over.

I shake my head. *I don't think so*, I say.

Josslyn lived alone?

I think, I say.

The Dominican man, whose name I now know is Luis, has told me, through a combination of hand motions, English, and Spanish, that they think the man who killed her might have been her son.

I leave the girls with their iPad and with Luis and I call my husband to tell him what's gone on.

Jesus, he says.

I think I'll start to cry but I stare straight ahead, wishing he were here, waiting for him to tell me what to do.

Did someone call her family? he says.

I think.

How are the girls?

Watching Dora, I say. I'm so grateful for the straightforward ways that comfort can be given to small children. *Eating junk food and being doted on.*

How are you? he says.

I stay quiet because we can't afford for him to hear me crying. If I start to cry he might come home and then we'll have no way to pay our rent.

The explosion makes the news and three of my friends call.

You have to move, says my friend who is quadrilingual.

We can't move, I don't say.

At the apartment, the burned smell is everywhere—the scorch of the explosion and the remnants of the water that they'd sprayed to make it stop, antiseptic smelling, bleachlike. It's proof, each time we walk up the stairs, that the memory of violence that runs through my head a thousand times a day is real. The girls' legs are small and squat and they're exhausted by the walk up six flights to the apartment. *Carry me,* they both say. On the third floor, I scoop one into each arm and keep going.

Three days straight, I call in sick to work: I pick them up early from school. I take them to the park and pack loads of snacks and we run around and have a picnic. The fountains at the playgrounds have been turned on and they get soaking wet, still in their clothes, and then fall asleep in the stroller as we walk home.

The four-year-old is too big maybe for the stroller, but with the stroller, I can run them, and we go all over town. I push them uphill, leaning forward, arms stretched straight and legs digging in.

We loiter at the bookstore and sit on the floor and I read to them. They ask to buy books but I explain this is the books' home and that they have to stay for now. They pile on top of me, one and then the other, each with a stack of books beside them. Our legs all stick together until someone's leg is taking up too much space and then there's fighting, and then both of them get up and my legs are wet from sweat. I ignore the emails from work. I think maybe I'll never go back and we'll tell the landlord that we're not paying rent until the apartment doesn't smell like smoke any longer, and then I think about Josslyn and I cry and then stop crying so our girls don't get scared.

I keep trying to fit it into my brain. We sat outside together drinking coffee, all the *hi hello kiss the girls how are yous*. She was a human who was loved and living. She died in this awful, thoughtless way. Like with nearly every other tragic thing I scroll through, in all the scrolling, I feel wholly ill equipped to digest it properly. I force myself, each time we climb the steps, to think about her, to attempt to mourn her, grieve her in some way. I try to hold, each time we walk past her door, the fact of her, and then I try to hold inside my head the fact of her being gone. I don't know, though, what to do with this fact. The specific shape this sadness takes is knobbed and awkward. We did not know her, really. The violence she experienced is almost unfathomable to me.

My husband comes home two days later. He got in a fight with his clients. He was desperate to come home and they refused to pay him because the job wasn't done but he still left. *Fuck them*, he says, when he talks about it, but he looks down. Our funds are dwindling. Later, after we've put the girls to bed, after they have hugged him, kissed him, climbed overtop him and he has cooked us dinner, we click through the spreadsheets we've been keeping to keep track of our income and our spending. His student loans weren't covered by the bankruptcy; we have piles of letters from creditors, one of whom is contesting the bankruptcy, and we have to pay the lawyer more. My husband says: *How is it we do everything so wrong?*

We have to dress up and get a babysitter.

We can't afford a babysitter, I say.

We can't afford not to go, my husband says.

We also can't afford this dinner if we have to pay our share. This man for whom my husband built six walls of bookshelves on the Upper West Side wants to talk to him about *some other opportunities*. We have seventy-two dollars in our bank account. Once we pay the babysitter we'll have none. We have to go because my husband has begun to think that maybe he should opt back in to the systems we decided to opt out of, and this guy might offer him a job, might offer him a way back in.

I put on mascara and a dress, then take it off and put on a black turtleneck and black pants and wash my face. I'm warier of looking like I've tried too hard and failing than I am of seeming like I don't care what they think. The children play in their room and I go in and read them books while my husband gets dressed.

The sitter comes and I hold the children's faces, kiss them. The baby quickly nurses. They're fresh from the bath and their hair's wet and they pile overtop me. *I don't want to go*, I say to no one. *Come on*, my husband says, from the hallway by the door. The building still smells like smoke. We walk down all the flights of stairs.

Who are these people again? I ask on the subway.

He has a start-up, says my husband. I think maybe it's my fault for saying all those years ago that he should do the thing he wanted. I think the thing that he was proud of, we were, his not being like them, has begun to feel less like what he wanted. We're both tired of being broke all of the time.

Right, I say.

Fuck start-ups, I say. After, we're quiet for a while.

The ads on the train are for a freelance website that I've never been on. They espouse the power of working nonstop, entrepreneurship. Before I got this job at the high school, I had five jobs and my husband had two and that's when we went a hundred thousand dollars in debt.

I hate this fucking ad campaign, I say to my husband.

I've said this before so he just nods.

Try not to swear this much at dinner, he says.

The people that we meet are our age. It takes me a minute to place her, but she sat next to me at the party on Long Island, held the baby's foot while I nursed her, months ago.

The guy says my husband's name but only part of it, like they're buddies. It's the same name my husband's friends from college use when we have awkward dinners with them at our house so we don't have to split the bill.

The woman goes in to kiss me, but I realize too late and pull away from her and she looks down. *I'm sorry*, I say. She's pretty. She has long, dark hair and dark-red lipstick, large earrings, and her eyes are lined.

She's a corporate lawyer, I remember.

That's so wonderful, she says, when I tell her I teach at the high school.

I really love the kids, I say.

Of course, she says. As if it is so generous of me. *Of course you do,* she says.

I wonder if this is all we'll say the whole night.

How are your little girls? she says.

Good, I say. *Magic,* I say. Relieved she brought them up.

We're still trying, she says, leaning close to me. I like her better up close. I see her want in the way her eyes dip closer to her nose; I smell it, desperate and sour, on her breath and lips.

On the menu I see that there is not a single meal that costs less than all the money we have sitting in our bank account.

I get a gin martini and my husband gets a whiskey and I register that, if we have to pay for our half, we are already close to having spent too much.

I talk about our kids while our drinks are delivered. I love talking about our kids and I show her pictures of them on my phone. My face heats up as I drink more and I'm sorry for her as she leans close to me.

How long have you been trying? I ask.

She touches the rim of her martini glass with a manicured finger. *Two years?* she says.

I touch her elbow and then wonder if I shouldn't.

I'm thirty-five, she says.

I'm younger than her but don't say this.

My best mom friend had her first kid at forty, I say. This is true, and she smiles, holds her hand over her mouth.

We get a shared plate of hors d'oeuvres and now we officially cannot afford this dinner. I drink more quickly. My drink is empty and we all get another round. I'm drunk already because I never drink because I'm still nursing.

I watch her stare at my husband as he talks.

You live in Brooklyn? she says. I tell her the name of our neighborhood. *Nice,* she says, nods.

Someone was murdered in our building, I say without thinking. She looks confused, then shocked, then scared. I tell her the whole story, thrilled, somehow, to watch the shape of it on her face. I feel both more separate and closer to both her and Josslyn as I go on.

Did they catch him? she says. *Will you stay there?*

We can't afford to move, I say, and shrug.

She drinks more and I tell her that they caught the guy within hours of his fleeing the building. They know now he was a stranger, not her son.

They think he's schizophrenic, I say. *His face and hands were burned.*

How awful, she says.

I'm breathless by the end and flushed and then I'm very sorry. I stand up to go to the bathroom and spend five minutes in a stall so I don't cry. I want to go home and lie down quiet in bed with our girls until they're grown.

When I come back my food has been served and is wilting. Everyone looks anxious, waiting, their napkins spread across their laps, food untouched.

You okay? my husband whispers.

Yeah, I say. I touch my glass's rim like she did.

We have a proposition, the guy says once I've sat and sliced into the steak but not yet chewed it. I look down at my food. I drop my fork, reach for my drink.

Okay, my husband says. *Go on*.

When we get home I've been crying and my husband's angry and my phone's dead in my pocket and both girls are deep asleep in bed. The babysitter is watching TV on her computer and my husband goes to pay her. I sit on the edge of one of the cribs we converted to beds and watch them sleep and cry a little more.

I grab hold of their feet; I kiss them; I find my husband in bed. They want, it turns out, not his skills or smarts or any of the kind of long-term employment that we had hoped for. They've offered us twenty thousand dollars for my husband's sperm.

It's raining the next morning, and I put on a long-sleeved shirt and shorts and wrap my phone inside a plastic bag so I can bring it with me. The rain's torrential and I don't see a single other person; it's still dark out. Water sloshes in my shoes and I have to wipe it from my eyes so I can see. Sometimes, as my feet fall into puddles, I wonder if I've misjudged their depth and my calves and thighs clench, just before my feet meet ground again and they take off.

I take my clothes off in the hall of our apartment when I get home. I leave a wet pile outside our front door, socks and shoes and shirt and shorts, and I peel off my sports bra and my underwear inside the bathroom as it fills with steam from the shower and I get in.

My husband grabs hold of my bare arm as I'm walking toward our room to get dressed with a towel wrapped around me.

You went running, he says.

I nod and shrug and smile.

His hand is big and warm but my arm stays tight and I start to lean away from him. He's not angry, but his grip also isn't soft.

This shutting down and pushing through, he says. *It's not as convincing as you think.*

There is a woman in Josslyn's apartment. The door is cracked open and I see her in the kitchen, opening the drawers.

Hello? I say.

It's been a month. The place still sits empty. Pieces of the floor tiles are still missing and the molding at the base of the hall walls close to her door is still charred.

Hi, says the woman in Josslyn's apartment.

She's my age, a little younger. She wears a pleated skirt, a tucked-in tank top, her hair held back in a bun. Last I heard from Luis, the cops think it was a random man who'd fixated on her from across the street for months.

I'm Iffy, she says.

I tell her my name.

Ifeoma, she says. *My name's Ifeoma, but my mom's the only one who calls me that.*

I nod.

There's a small box a quarter full in the corner, an old TV on a wooden box in front of a dark-red couch with a wool blanket spread over the back in the room past where she stands.

Josslyn was my mom, she says.

I'm so sorry, I say.

I think I want to hug her but stay still.

She nods, her hands still by her sides. *She was a little nuts,* she tells me.

She shakes her head and I step closer to her but stop at Josslyn's doorway.

She says, again: *She was my mom.*

I'm at work when I get an email from the rich woman. There are paragraphs below her signature about copyright and confidentiality. The disclaimer covers ten times the space of the few sentences she writes.

I worry that we shocked you, she writes, *and I'm sorry. I hope you don't mind I found your email online. I wanted to say that we don't mean to presume anything in our asking for this thing that feels so monumental. It's just we liked your husband so much. We're so desperate to find something that works.*

Everybody likes my husband, is attracted to him; everybody falls in love with him.

She tells me about their failed attempts at IVF and her husband's low sperm count. She tells me she's imagined inserting the sperm of someone she doesn't know into her womb. *They clean it,* she writes. *In a machine. It's all so strange and clinical and I couldn't quite imagine how a baby might come out in the end. It's all so abstract, so unreal, so exactly nothing like I thought. I just,* she says. *I thought it would be worth it to ask and I am sorry if it freaked you out.*

I sit at the high school in an office with five other people. Fake wood panels separate our desks. Everyone seems always to be busy. I used to feel busy, but now I come here and stare at my computer, not sure how I used to fill all of my time. I keep looking around to see if anyone is watching. I wonder if someone somewhere in human resources has gotten an alert because the word *sperm* passed through the network on its way to me.

I close my computer and go back to reading: *So Big*, Edna Ferber. *About mistakes it's funny. You've got to make your own; and not only that, if you try to keep other people from making theirs they get mad.*

I pretend the woman hasn't emailed. I want to be able to say no to her without thinking. I want to give her what she wants, to get what we want, and not care. I no longer believe that there's such a thing as everybody getting what they want and no one paying for it later. I'm embarrassed, maybe, by how much I still hope that we can get to okay on our own.

I'm sorry if it freaked you out, I think.

I call Melissa to check in about the investigation, to see if she's in trouble. She says she hasn't heard from anyone. *Which means*, she tells me, *that I'm the one under investigation for whatever they think I did.*

Some fucking shit, I say.

I know, she says. It's all politics.

There are factions in the department of which I have very little knowledge—groups of people allied with one another who like to hire other allies. Groups of people who have, for a long time, been trying to push her out.

I leave work early and surprise our girls at pickup.

Mommy, says the four-year-old, on our walk home, *if you don't go to work, will we still live?*

The Chilean writer's going home for a month before the start of the new semester. She calls and I'm supposed to be at work but I'm staring at a painting in a gallery in the East Village by myself; it's a landscape, Rackstraw Downes, the city; it's all the sketches that he drew in advance. I'm not sure, after telling her all that I told her, that I can be in the same room with her again, but I see her name and I answer, wanting then to tell her about what I'm looking at.

I'll come meet you, she says, before I can stop her.

The paintings are just shy of realist: meticulously detailed and from unexpected angles.

We're not far from Chinatown, and we walk farther south to get a plate of dumplings.

I've missed you, she says, holding my arm; I feel my body lean toward hers.

I talk less than she talks and she doesn't mention Sasha.

My sister, she says. *The one who's dead.*

The dumplings are filled with pork and beef. The salt settles on my tongue and I have to open my full mouth to let the heat out.

We took her youngest daughter in after she died.

I wrap my hands around my green tea.

She was fourteen and her brothers were all older. She found her, her mother; she'd strung herself up by her neck.

My son was still in the house and, though maybe I didn't know it then, my marriage was ending. And we took this feral girl into our house because I thought maybe I had killed her mother. We took her, I guess, because she had nowhere else to go.

She was wild, she says. *Dumbstruck, maybe. She hardly knew us; her dad was gone, her mother dead.*

It was awful, she says, *for the months and years that followed. I was watching her destroy herself in slow motion. We tried all the systems, all the techniques, all the private schools and therapists and locking her inside her room, and nothing worked.*

But time passed, she said. *She got older. Time passing is the only truth I believe in anymore.*

We're not friends now, she says. *She doesn't call me Mom or tell me that she loves me. But she has thanked us once or twice for caring for her. She finished college, has a small apartment not far from us. Once a month or so she agrees to come over for a meal.*

I love her, she says, *and I think my sister would be grateful for it. I'm grateful that I get to love her, that there is that space still, for me to make a sort of amends.*

I get coffee with the rich woman who wants to buy my husband's sperm. I touch my stomach while we talk, unthinking. I do this all the time and it's only now—cognizant, suddenly, of my powers as a baby maker in the presence of this woman who seems so wholly defined by her inability to make a baby—that I realize how often I do this.

Can't you get sperm for cheaper? I want to say. *Aren't there better ways to spend your money? What is it like,* I want to ask, *to have money like you do?* I can't fathom the power, the way she must walk around every day so differently than I do. *What's it like,* I want to say, *to have pain in your teeth and go get them fixed instead of waiting it out until you're pretty sure the nerve has died since you don't feel it any longer? To not always have to be shortsighted because to look ahead is to just see more and more, but even more expensive, of the same? To not get the bad, refurbished phone that you have to replace regardless, the winter coats and hats and gloves that fall apart and break?* I can fathom this, because I used to have it, because I was brought up inside it and had to unlearn it, which makes me resent it that much more. I recognize the look of it on other people, and I hate them, because I still have to remind myself, too often, that what they have is no longer mine.

I'm not so very married to genetics, I say. *But I'm not sure this is my choice.*

Your husband said you needed to be okay with it, she says. *That's what he told Jeremy.*

I have forgotten that her husband's name is Jeremy.

I am momentarily furious that my husband talked to him without my knowing, but I appreciate—though, of course, also resent—that he has given me the final say.

I want everything both ways all the time and I'm tired of feeling sorry for this. I want the money that they would give us and for my husband to be okay with it, for us to just forget about it, to pretend it never happened, to pay our rent for a few months without worry. But I have no control over my thoughts or feelings, and the fact that somewhere in the world would be a small baby like our babies, who is part of him but who we cannot love and keep safe, who we cannot check on late at night when she is sleeping, makes me scared and sad.

The rich woman says: *I feel hollow all the time.*

I can't look at her. She is a person who has lost things, who has felt things. I don't have space left in my brain to worry about her too.

I'm sorry, I say.

I liked you so much, she says, *the night we met.*

I think how good I am at pretending.

Jeremy said things haven't been easy for you guys, she says.

My hand is, once again, on my stomach. *Fuck you*, I think.

Jeremy says your husband says you're miserable at your job. We could offer you— she says.

I think she is about to offer us an amount of money that

we could not say no to, and I almost reach up as if to place my hand over her mouth.

When I leave her I walk an hour before getting on the subway. As we wait underground, because the train's delayed, I scroll through to Sasha's Instagram and then I see her: squished face, thick, dark patch of hair, and mottled skin. Sasha's baby. And Sasha smiling, her face perfect, holding her.

6

THERE ARE ONLY two weeks left of school and everyone has mostly stopped pretending that they have a job to do. Everyone has stopped pretending they know how.

I went into the meeting in which I was meant to get my offer for the next school year and the principal ate grilled cheese. He showed me a contract with a two percent raise and told me he thought I was more well suited to teach ninth grade, though I've been teaching the juniors and seniors all year, though I was hired to help to prep the upperclassmen for college.

I told him I wasn't sure kids that young would be the best fit for me.

My background is university teaching, I said.

He nodded, already knew this, wiped tomato off his face.

Ninth grade doesn't take any tests, though, he said. *I know,* he said, *test prep isn't your thing.*

A week later, I went back into his office and I quit.

There are people I like who are staying, or who are finding jobs at other schools like ours. Both my co–homeroom teachers plan on leaving also, one for grad school, one for another school. I think briefly of thanking them for covering for me, all those times that I was absent, but then I'd have to tell them that I left and so stay quiet. I look down at the floor each time I tell another person that I'm leaving. I pick at the edge of whatever shirt I'm wearing and give some heartfelt, earnest talk about the system being broken. But it won't get better when I leave it. I'm leaving because I love my students but not as much as I wish I loved them, not enough to work harder and be better; because I love my children more.

I'll be paid through the summer and, with Melissa's help, I've picked up three more adjunct jobs for the next semester. We cannot live outside the systems and the structures, but, it turns out, I cannot live within them either anymore.

There are murmurings—they've reached a higher pitch this past month—that the corporation to which we send our rent check is going to take the opportunity of Josslyn's death to turn the apartments in our building into co-ops. I sleep later and later and my runs get shorter. I eat the free junk food at work and feel lethargic and my clothes start to feel tight. I am no longer willing to have sex with my husband. This does not happen all at once, and I still sometimes give in. But each time he reaches for me—I can't stop thinking about that asshole professor at my night class, every man I see each time I read the news—my skin crawls and I want to hide in the corner of the bed and go to sleep.

It's complicated, I say, when he looks at me.

I just can't right now, I say.

It's not complicated that you don't want me, he says.

It's not about you, I say.

Except it is, he says.

It's men, I say. *I don't want to give anything to any man right now.*

He's a good husband and this isn't fair. I understand this. And yet I still don't want to. Sometimes I give into it because I want him to be happy, because I love him and I like him and he's a good dad and he loves me. I curl even closer to the wall afterward.

Every morning, before school, I meet Kayla and I buy her breakfast at the diner across the street from school. She texted me from the train to school three months ago that she was hungry and she was early and I offered to get her food. We met here and then again the next day. I get coffee and she gets a four-dollar sausage, egg, and cheese, and we sit and talk or we are quiet and she eats. I sip my coffee with extra milk and try hard not to put my arm around her as we walk to school.

Be careful there, says my co–homeroom teacher as she watches Kayla and me walk through security together, laughing.

I am, I tell her, without wholly knowing what she's saying, knowing that whatever line she's warning I not cross is long since past.

I've texted Sasha *Congrats* even though she didn't tell me. *Thanks,* she responds a day later, another emoji, and I want to call or go to her, but I can't, so I just wait for her to call and every day, when she still hasn't, I check again for pictures but there's none. I see the same one she posted twice more, posted by her mother and her sister, and, late at night, I stare at her, click through each version, wondering what she's like.

———

I get home from work late because it's the end of the year and I'm starting to realize I won't ever see my students again after the year ends. I give them my number and my nonwork email just in case. I think I'll hear from Kayla, one or two of the others—the kids off to college, the ones I have promised to help with their freshman-year papers if they give me enough advance warning, will send me some late-night emails at the end of each semester the first year. We sit together in a classroom after their finals and I help them with their personal statements; the CEO won't let them go home for summer until drafts of their statements are turned in. I have candy in my bag from the teacher workroom, and I hand it out to the six or so kids who sit with me. I have each of them read their statement out loud and we try to make sense of them together. One girl writes about a summer program she went to and how she ran out of money. Her father had saved so that she could have some spending money while she was there—except, she writes in the statement, she was with these other kids who spent money like there was no end to money. It was a three-week program. She had seven dollars left at the end of the first week. She writes about calling her dad and asking him to send her more and the way she was transported back to her life as she listened to him, silent on the other end for too long. How quickly she'd forgotten the image of her parents, who worked on their feet all day, her dad a mechanic, her mom braiding hair. He sent the money to her. She forced herself to envision, she writes in the statement, what they had gone without, done more of, to make that possible. Another boy writes about asking questions, his obsession with it; another boy writes about cooking dinner for his mom, and then about a trip he took with Outward Bound. I help them to fix sentences and sharpen paragraphs. We laugh and their work starts to get better and I think maybe I should stay.

My boss comes around hours after we've started working. It's the last day of school and a week since finals; a lot of kids either did not come or have long since left. My boss, who likes to be the center of attention, comes in and asks what we're doing, why my students aren't in their other classes. They're juniors and I haven't been their teacher now for months. *We don't have other classes*, says one of them. *She's helping us.* He looks at me, then looks at them, and says, eyes back on me, *You know she's leaving you next year. She tell you yet that she's not coming back?*

They nod and know although I haven't told them. I've been too afraid to tell them. They know, though, because so few of their teachers last more than a year. They've had years of learning not to ever get attached to anyone at school. I wish again, sitting with them, that I could be the exception, that I could be one of the few who stays for them. I've chosen not to, just like nearly everyone who looked like me who came before me. I wish I could explain that they're the only thing about this place worth sticking around for. I imagine, watching all these teachers come and go so quickly—they're children—it must still feel at least a little—they're wrong, but I don't think they could help but think it—like their fault.

I take the subway home. I read *LaRose*, by Louise Erdrich. Our girls are with my husband, so I walk into a bar close to our house and get a gin drink. I get out my book, but then I see Josslyn's daughter. *Ifeoma*, I say in my head twice before saying it to her—I've googled it and listened to it pronounced back to me by the computer—wanting very much to say it right.

Hey, she says. *I forgot your name.*

I tell her.

Right, she says. *Hi.*

I didn't know you were still here, I say.

I got an Airbnb close by, she says. *I'm trying to sell all of my mom's stuff. Find some way to bring the rest of it back down south with me.*

Where do you live? I say.

Atlanta, she says.

I've only been there once, I say.

She smiles.

I almost tell her I'm from Florida, except Florida's not the real South. Where I'm from is more like a weird, debased New York or New Jersey with a beach. *You like it?* I say.

Sure, she says. *I grew up here and always wanted to leave.*

Here, here? I say, meaning this neighborhood, this building.

Yup, she says.

How was that? I say.

She's a nurse practitioner and went to a specialty high school in the neighborhood for science.

Mom wanted me to be a doctor, she says. *But I got tired.*

She was . . . I start. *I'm so sorry about what happened.*

You didn't do anything, she says.

But, you know, I say. *She was always so kind to me,* I say. As if this matters.

Me too, she says.

I want to ask if she knows any more about what happened. I have this impulse to try to make sense of every tragedy, as if that is the way I will stay safe.

She made me lasagna when our kids were born, I say.

Oh god, she says. *I hope you threw it away.*

I laugh and nod. *I did,* I say.

She couldn't eat lactose, she says. *She cooked everything with rubber cheese. She'd lost it a little*, she says. *She was lonely.*

You have siblings? I say, though I already know the answer.

Two brothers out west, she says. *Neither of whom, like these assholes thought for a while, was the one who hurt my mom.*

Did they come out? I say.

We all fought a lot, she says.

We all get selfish, I say. *Or get so set on doing everything the way we want.*

I called her, she says. *Every Sunday.*

I'm sure she loved that, I say.

She nods. *She said she did.*

I have unthinkingly, shamefacedly, invited Kayla for dinner. She has mentioned that she's home alone and even though I know she'll come from far away, that she'll have to take the train home late at night, I want to have her at our house.

She texts to say, *Is it okay if I bring my brother?*

Sure, I say. I don't tell my husband, until right before they get there and our girls are about to go to bed.

She's bringing her brother, I say.

How old is he? says my husband.

Five, I say.

It's a school night, he says.

This was all a terrible idea—presumptuous boundary crossing—but now I can't take it back.

Kayla wears more makeup than she does at school. Her dress is short and her hair is done in long, tight braids. Her brother holds on tight to her and doesn't look at me as I let them into the building and lead them up to our apartment. He still wears his uniform from school, is round-faced, stocky. His shoes are Velcro like our girls'.

The girls are brimming, anxious; *Who's here, who's here,* they say, wet haired, teeth brushed, bed ready.

Mommy's friend, my husband says.

My student, I correct him.

They look at Kayla's brother first, about their size. He keeps his face turned toward Kayla's leg as she grins and leans down to hug each of the girls.

How was the train? asks my husband.

Kayla laughs and I'm relieved to hear her laugh and the girls look at her. *Long,* she says.

My husband laughs as well.

Our girls lead them into the small room off the kitchen where we all just barely fit. A small couch that sits two or three, two grown-up chairs around the kitchen table, two small, old IKEA chairs for kids.

I have to pee, says Kayla's brother.

I'll take you, says the four-year-old and grabs hold of him.

He starts at her but lets her hold his hand.

He's adorable, I say to Kayla when they've walked toward the bathroom.

So are they, she says.

My husband gets the dinner from the stove and the table's already been set and I get all of us a glass of water and Kayla answers questions from the two-year-old about her shoes and dress.

How's school? asks my husband, perhaps because he doesn't listen when I tell him what the school's like, perhaps because he's not sure what else to ask a teenager.

It's fine, Kayla says.

I try to remember what we talk about at school, but we're not at school.

She teach you anything? my husband asks.

I'm not her teacher, I say.

She's taught me things, Kayla says, and I feel my face turn red.

The four-year-old and Kayla's brother come back, their hands wet from the sink, and sit on the couch playing with the magnet tiles the girls have brought out from their room.

You hungry? I say to the boy.

He shakes his head.

He doesn't talk much if he doesn't know you, Kayla says.

He talks to me, the four-year-old says.

Kayla laughs. *That's good,* she says.

It's late and I can feel my husband getting anxious. If the girls don't get to bed soon, they'll begin to disassemble. The four-year-old will pass tiredness and start spinning, scaling the furniture, impossible to calm down. The two-year-old will start to cry and not stop.

You want to take him to go play? I say to the four-year-old.

She takes the boy's hand and they both run down the hall into her and her sister's bedroom.

The two-year-old watches briefly, her eyes bleary. *Can I sit on your lap?* she says. I think that she means me, but just as I say yes, I watch as Kayla lifts her.

You're good with kids, my husband says.

Kayla nods. *Some of them,* she says.

Yeah, he says. *Some aren't great.*

She smiles.

The two-year-old has hold of one of her braids and runs it back and forth through each of her fingers.

Baby, I start to say, reaching for her. But Kayla shakes her head and tells me that it's fine.

What grade are you in? asks my husband.

Tenth, says Kayla.

You know what you want to do?

I realize that I've never asked her.

Psychology, she says.

Makes sense, my husband says.

I wonder if she thinks I told him about her slipping out of class, her leaving. I haven't, though I'm not sure why.

I want to understand why people do the things they do, she says.

You'd be good at it, I say.

We hear a scream from the kids' room. I get up and go to them and Kayla follows.

Kayla's brother sits on the floor in tears and the four-year-old stands holding three stuffed animals.

What happened? I say.

They're special to me, she says.

You have to share, I say. *We have a guest and you need to share.*

I watch as her lip trembles. Kayla has hold of her brother and he's slowly calming down.

Which one do you want to play with? I say to him. He nods toward a purple octopus our four-year-old is clutching fiercely.

Kiddo, I say, *give it to him.*

She shakes her head more surely, her teeth grabbing hold of her lip.

Hey, says Kayla, looking toward her from her brother. Her voice sounds different, sweeter, softer. *I have an idea,* she says, to the four-year-old, *come here.*

The four-year-old looks back and forth between us, toys still clutched to her, teeth still clamped overtop her lip.

Come here, Kayla says again.

She walks to her slowly, eyes on her little brother. Kayla

pulls her closer still and whispers to her. I watch her let her lip loose. I watch the corners of her mouth turn up.

The four-year-old nods as Kayla finishes talking. The four-year-old hands Kayla's brother two of the toys and smiles at him.

Sorry, she says.

He mumbles back to her and grabs hold of the two toys and they go back to playing.

You're so good, I say.

Kayla laughs. *I know*, she says.

We've finished dinner and the two-year-old nurses on my lap. My husband gives Kayla and her brother a couple of the cookies that he baked with our girls and suggests he order them a car.

I don't know what to say and so stay quiet. A car from here to where she lives would be close to a hundred dollars.

You sure? says Kayla.

My husband looks at her brother, chewing on his cookie, our four-year-old close to him still, asking if he wants to come again to play with her. I know as soon as they leave she will cry on the floor because he's gone and it will be hours before we get her to sleep.

Of course, says my husband. *You have school.*

We don't have a hundred dollars that we won't miss. I'm grateful to him for not caring. I hug Kayla and her brother goodbye and we all sit out on our stoop together, quiet, as we wait for the car.

I can't do it, says the text from Sasha when I find my phone and bring it into bed to scroll through, after the hour and a half we spent convincing the children it was time for sleeping, after I lay in bed with the two-year-old and then her sister, after we read six books each and they cried and we rubbed their backs and sang them songs.

I don't know how, she says.

I stare at her text, thinking maybe I should ask my husband. *I don't either*, I think.

You can, I type back, then delete it. I think I should call her, but then I take the phone back from my ear and try to type the perfect text. I delete all of them, and my husband's passed out beside me and the two-year-old has woken up and cries again, asking to come sleep with us, so I go get her and I nurse her and once she's asleep again and exhaling hot breath against my side as she sleeps, I text back: *You can*.

I can't stay here, she says, immediately.

What's wrong? I ask.

I'm bad at it, she says. The dots pop up, then disappear, then pop up, then disappear. I sit up in the bed and accidentally knock the baby. She starts and murmurs, then grabs hold of my arm and settles back again.

No one's good at it, I say.

I can't lose her too, she says.

What can I do? I say.

7

I THOUGHT MAYBE she would ask for me to come and I could help her. I could hold the baby and we could take care of her together. We could do what we should have done before. I wasn't up for it then, maybe we both weren't, but I think I know how now; I could make all of it better, if only I still believed that there was such a thing as making it better after all. I want to go to her and meet her husband, hug her, hug the baby, hold her while she takes a shower, do her laundry; I could bring her dinner, to be friends just like I'm friends with other people, where no one expects more than whatever you can give. Two days later, I get a text as her plane lands at JFK and she gets in a cab to our apartment. *Five minutes away.* I don't know who she tells before she comes, who she's left with the baby. *I'm by myself,* she texts. I'm sweating and I keep looking at my face in the mirror of our tiny bathroom. I keep running my hands through my hair and wondering if I will hug her without realizing I've hugged her, wondering if I might finally be able to give her what she needed all those years ago.

SHE'S HER BUT not her: bloated, splotched skin, no makeup; her hair up and unkempt; still beautiful. I look down furtively to see if there's a car seat that I somehow missed, if she brought the baby with her. I look at her abdomen, wondering if the baby was made up.

Hey, I say.

All that talking, years of reading: There was a time I thought that all language might contain something of value, but most of life is flat and boring and the things we say are too. Or maybe it's that most of life is so much stranger than language is able to make room for, so we say the same dead things and hope maybe the who and how of what is said can make it into what we mean.

She looks like she might melt, she might disassemble in our hallway. I think I should pick her up, carry her into our room and hold her, rub her back until she falls asleep.

I almost hug her but I stay standing in the doorway.

I like the place, she says.

Come in, I say, backing away.

Is something burning? she says, having still not come in.

I look past her to Josslyn's door.

My husband's working. The girls are home but with the babysitter.

Who's here, Mommy? they both yell. They come running out of their bedroom.

The four-year-old grabs Sasha's hand and tries to pull her into her room. *You want to play with us?* she says.

Mariah, I say, to the babysitter.

Guys, I say.

Sasha's started crying. Our four-year-old still holds her hand and tells her crying is how your body gets the sad out and it's fine.

The babysitter scoops them back into their room.

You want coffee? I say. *Water?* I look through the pantry. *Gin?*

These are the only beverages I have on hand. She looks up at me from underneath a tent of hair; she says, *Water would be great*.

I hand her a glass, not meeting her eyes, not wanting to make her cry harder. I see stains popping on either side of her shirt and realize that her breasts are leaking. I nod toward her chest. *You want to use my pump?*

She looks down.

Fuck, she says.

I get the hand pump from the bathroom and the electric pump from our bedroom just to give her options. She nods toward the electric pump, which does both breasts at once, and I twist the bottles onto the horns for her while she sips her water and I plug the machine into the wall.

Such a fucking mess, she says.

She pulls her shirt up and I see she doesn't have a bra on. Her belly has that wore-out, saggy look of having held a baby recently.

The pump starts its whir and I see her breathe. The milk drops into the bottles, filling slowly. I pour myself a glass of water and sit at the kitchen table while she sits on the couch so I don't accidentally rub her back.

How was the trip? I say.

Long.

I don't want to ask about the baby, but we can hear my babies, playing, laughing; the four-year-old yells at her sister and both Sasha and I smile and then she starts to cry again.

They're so big, she says.

I know, I say, shaking my head.

They look like you, she says.

I stand up and walk over to the couch and I take the horns from her so I can screw the caps onto the bottles as she wipes herself. I bring the apparatus over to the sink to wash it while she pulls her shirt down, sips more water, sits back on the couch. I put the bottles in the fridge.

It's cold, she says. She did not have a coat when she got here.

I wasn't really thinking, she says. *When I left.*

What were you . . . I say.

Are you okay? I ask.

She looks at me. This was a stupid question.

I hear the babysitter yell out the name of our two-year-old as she opens up their bedroom door and waddles, quickly, toward me. *Milk?* she says, reaching underneath my shirt.

Not now, baby, I say.

Please, mama, she says.

I don't mind, says Sasha.

The two-year-old takes this as assent enough and climbs up onto my lap as Sasha watches. I unhook my bra and let her latch on, calling to the babysitter that it's fine.

I watch Sasha seem to reach for the baby's foot, then stop.

It's so mammalian, she says.

I laugh. I say: *It is.*

How old is she?

Two, I say.

And the other one? she says. She knows her name, I think, and I wonder why she doesn't name her.

She's four.

What's four like? she says.

Magic, I say, without thinking. *So much language. She's such a person,* I say.

I think both our brains think briefly about the baby who would now be ten.

Yeah, she says. Eyes still on the baby's feet.

I want to shift the conversation to her. I want to make sure, while knowing there's no way that this is possible, that she's okay.

Your . . . I start. "Baby," "marriage," "life" are all the words that flit through my head as awful stand-ins for the part of her right now that I am most concerned about. *Did you . . .*

Can we just sit a while? she says.

My husband comes home and makes all of us dinner.

He hugs her and I'm so grateful for him, this man who's good and kind and sees clearly she's been crying.

How are you? she says to him, more earnest than I would have thought.

I'm fine, he says, gesturing toward the squealing children and the mess of our apartment. *Chaos.*

She laughs and I love him in a million different ways from how I did when he hugged her, in a million different ways from how I loved him when she met him that first time, years ago.

At dinner, the four-year-old gives us a ten-minute tutorial on chinchillas and then performs, with her sister, how high they jump in the Andes Mountains, where, she says, they live. The two-year-old tells Sasha about playing on the swings at recess with her friends. My husband talks about the house he's working on that has a cave and waterfall attached to the backyard pool. She stays mostly quiet, asking the girls questions, smiling at me as I cut their food, clean up spilled water, share my seltzer with the baby when she asks.

I watch her watch them and think how obscenely lucky I am. I am touching, the whole time, the baby, then her sister, then my husband, as I walk past him to get the four-year-old more food.

My husband bathes them and she and I sit together on the couch and she asks more questions about our lives now. I tell her, briefly, about work.

I make up a bed for her on the couch in the back room close to the girls' room. *I have nowhere else*, I start to say, but think it might be worse, apologizing for putting her so close to our kids. I wonder if I should call her husband. I think I have her sister's number. I could send him a message on Instagram, or post a picture of her, tag her in it, let him know she's safe.

I climb up into our bed, where my husband reads.

Is she okay? he says.

I'm not sure.

He kisses me and I kiss him back in the way that tells him I'm not just saying good night. I lean toward him. We have sex with me on top for the first time in months and he falls asleep and I stare up at the ceiling, trying to listen for her breathing, until I finally drift off. At 2:00 am I wake him up and we have sex again. I run my hands up his back and chest and reposition myself and tell him to slow down and crawl off of him and push my back into his chest until he slips inside of me again. He holds his hands against my stomach and I rock into him and he comes and I do too. He kisses my forehead, and I laugh a minute later when I come back from the bathroom and he's already passed out.

Hours later, my husband's still asleep, sheets twisted at his feet, his boxers on, his shirt still off. I've wrapped myself in the duvet, burrowed in against the wall.

I think then that I'll go to her. *Talk to her*. I want to wake her up and sit with her, the children breathing so close by that we can hear.

I want to tell her that I'm sorry. That what I thought was friendship then was only needing from her, that the moment that she needed me I disappeared. I want to tell her that I left her by herself and that I shouldn't have; I left her twice. I should have gone back with her when she left that day in Asia, should have called her every day until she was all better, been there with her the whole time.

I want to go to her and tell her that I'm scared I'll never feel again the way I used to feel just standing next to her. I want to tell her that I'm scared I'm too wore out, worn down, that this constant anxious ache that I have now isn't about my job or kids or all the ways life isn't what it should be, that maybe it's just me, it's most of who I am. That I loved so much believing that there was such a thing as fixing, getting better. That knowing that's not true, that it's all just more of the same, exhausts me more than all those nights that I can't sleep, the miles that I run.

I want to throw all the words inside my head out into the room, and then to sit and listen to her. I want to sit, the two of us, and stitch them all together, into a string that makes not just sense but something better, bigger, surer than whatever they were, we were, before.

I want to tell her all of this, but in different words, or maybe somehow better, but when I hear the whir of the pump and climb down out of bed and it's still dark out, she's crying quietly, and I know there isn't space, not now, to say any of what I want.

I know there is this other thing I didn't know about a long time, the whole time that I knew her, this thing that feels both less and more than all that talk and want. It's what my children taught me, maybe, feeding, cleaning, changing, holding in the middle of the night when they can't sleep: love but less like saving, talking, more like doing, love where there's no other side and that's the part that's worst but also best.

I sit very close to her and I'm quiet and she starts to cry and I don't try to stop her. I hear the children breathe. The small plastic bottles fill, the drip drip of the milk goes on and we sit still. I take the bottles from her and I cap them. She wipes herself, pulls down her shirt. I take the plastic horns to wash in one hand, the bottles to put in the fridge. I stand up and she lies down and I go to put the bottles away, wash the horns and set them to dry on a towel on the counter. I climb back up to bed and lie still and do not sleep but listen to them—her, our girls, my husband; they turn and stir and I wait for them to wake up so the day can start.

SHE DRINKS COFFEE in the kitchen as we get ready. We pack lunches, make breakfast. The four-year-old says she has to *get the sleep out of my eyes* and lies in bed with the lights off and moans until I pick her up, blanket over her head, and carry her to the table to eat her oatmeal with cut-up fruit.

I have to pee, says the baby, two bites into her breakfast.

Okay, I say.

She looks at Sasha. *Will you come with me?*

She has a hard time climbing onto the toilet, I say.

Sasha smiles at her, clutches her coffee. *Sure,* she says.

She comes with me to drop the girls at school. I'm done already, but they have another couple of weeks. She holds the baby's hand and the baby asks Sasha if she has any children.

I do, she says.

The two-year-old looks at her, waiting.

A baby girl, says Sasha.

Can we play with her? asks the four-year-old.

Sure, Sasha says.

When?

Soon? she says.

We walk as if this hasn't happened. The four-year-old holds her hand and the two-year-old holds mine.

I ask questions about their sleep and their school day so they'll stop asking her things. I ask them their plans for the day, what they think they'll have for lunch.

Can you pick us up? the four-year-old asks Sasha.

She looks overtop both of them at me.

Maybe, I say. We walk them into their classrooms; I hug

them, kiss them. They hug her and she seems unsure where to put her limbs; her ears turn red.

I went to the hospital when they were really little, I say. *Right after the baby was born.*

We've been walking fifteen minutes. She wears the same clothes she wore the night before. Her hair's pulled back.

I was light-headed and fell over and it was scary. I put my symptoms in the computer and some big red box popped up that said, GO TO THE HOSPITAL.

She doesn't talk so I keep talking.

I'd gone running, then was nursing. The baby was eating every hour and she never slept.

We cross a busy street and I grab hold of her elbow without thinking. I think I feel her settle into me. Neither of us talks until we're on a quieter block.

I sat in a hospital bed and no one wanted or needed from me for eight whole hours and it was the calmest that I felt in months.

Were you okay? she asks me.

Fine, I say. *I mean, there was nothing diagnosably wrong.*

I wanted it for so long, she says.

It's scary, I say.

I finally have her and she's mine, but then—I kept thinking I didn't have a right to her, that I wasn't good for her, that I shouldn't be allowed . . .

None of us should be allowed, I say.

I think about her, she says. *The baby,* she says. *The other baby. All the time, I think about her. I think maybe I got to think that that's what being a mother is.*

It's part, I start to say.

I started to think that maybe all I could do was care about her, about both of them, from far away, that up close, I was a danger to them, that I would kill her also. That I would hurt her too somehow.

I know all the ways I'm supposed to stop her, but I don't.

I didn't really want her, she says. *I didn't know what I wanted,* she says. *I thought for years she died because I didn't want her like I should have wanted her.*

She looks over at me; her face grown-up, tired. *Sasha,* I think, *I am so sorry.*

You were so young, I say.

A fluke, she says. *A freak thing,* she says. *Cells and chromosomes misfiring. The sort of thing that could happen again.*

I stay quiet and I lean toward her. This baby is perfect, healthy. The first miscarriage was a freak thing. Her body was deemed, after, *perfect*. It doesn't make the fear feel any less.

I wouldn't survive it, she says.

I'm not sure I would either.

I can't, she says. *Again.*

We pass a basketball pavilion, a major street and a large crosswalk. A bus pulls up close to her and I grab her arm again and she starts and I let go and we walk so our shoulders almost touch.

The third week of our first baby's life, my mother came to see her. Nursing wasn't working. I was tired all the time. My breasts squirted milk too hard, too much, and the baby sputtered and choked as she was eating. She clamped down to stop the flow from coming and it hurt and I tensed up and she tensed up and both of us cried all day and night. *I'm waterboarding her,* I said to my husband. He would fall asleep, as if we should not, every second, be up and making sure that she was safe and happy. *How dare you,* I would think, and I'd feel far away and by myself. I broke out in hives and began to run a fever. I scratched the hives and they bled and I wore long sleeves in summer for the short periods of the day I was outside. I walked back and forth and up and down the halls of our apartment and I refused to give her anything but my breasts because the books I read and the internet said otherwise, I would have failed her, otherwise, I might not be good enough to have her after all. I kept gushing milk and she kept crying. I felt certain some higher authority would come take her. Instead, my mother: with enough clothes to clothe all of Brooklyn's babies, with blankets and garish plastic toys that lit up and made noise.

She's not okay, she whispered to my husband.

Is she seeing someone? she asked. She, who had never believed in seeing someone up till now.

I had been seeing someone, but I'd stopped when she was born.

Maybe she shouldn't be alone with her, she said, while I stood outside the kitchen and listened. I had not taken leave from school because then I would have lost my health insurance. I strapped her to me and nursed her in an office between classes as I continued to try to read and write and think.

My mother said, *She has a history.*

She's fine, my husband said. *She's tired.*

She needs to just give her a bottle, she said.

I cannot, he said, *tell her what to do*.

I walked out of the apartment, shaking. I left the baby. My breasts ached all of the time and leaked through my shirt. I had my keys and phone and I called Sasha and she answered though we hadn't spoken, then, in years. I think maybe I figured that she wouldn't answer but she answered.

It's so much, I said to her without preamble. She knew we

had a baby. She'd been on the mass email announcement. I hadn't known how to tell her about it besides that.

I don't, I said. *Sash.*

I knew as soon as she picked up I had no right to ask.

Breathe, she said.

My mom's here, I said.

Oof.

We laughed.

What if she takes her? I said.

She's yours, she said. *She can't take her.*

Both of us were quiet a long time then. I thought about the baby still not with her, the baby that she birthed but never had.

How did you . . . I started.

You're fine, she said. She would not, had never talked about it to me. *You are going to be fine,* she said.

I said her name and she said mine and I stood on the street with cars passing and people looking at me. I had no bra on and milk fell down into my waistband and my belly button and the skin below my abdomen still smarted from where they'd cut me open, just like they'd cut her open, days before.

Go home, she said.

I did.

You ever heard of the dive reflex? she says.

I shake my head. We're close now to our apartment and we pass the bar where I sat with Ifeoma, our laundromat.

It's biological, she says. She makes a face and I smile at her. There was a point when she'd bring up biology, when we were in high school and she loved biology and I loved books, and I'd yell at her to stop because I thought science made no sense.

It's a physiological response to immersion, she says. *Do you know what the homeostatic reflexes are?*

I shake my head.

It's the body's basic impulse to maintain homeostasis in response to stimuli, she says.

I only half know what she's saying, but I love the look and sound of her now, confident all of a sudden. I try not to bring my face too close to hers.

The body understands it's underwater, and it responds by redistributing oxygen to the most vital organs, the heart and brain, until it's able to come up for air again. There are sensory receptors in the nose that initiate the reflex when they fill with water, so then the body can stay under for longer than it should were we immersed without this.

She's broken free of my arm now and we're standing on a corner by our apartment and cars and people pass and I listen and she talks.

After, she says. *In med school. I was so mad at you then. But when I learned about this, I thought about you, about both of us. We were underwater. There was only so much oxygen.*

When we get back to the apartment, I ask her to show me pictures of the baby, and she shows me.

She takes her phone out.

I scroll through all the various squished-faced candids.

She watches me.

I smile at the tiny, shriveled thing.

She's beautiful, I say, which is not right, but close enough, and she nods and stares at her over my shoulder.

She starts crying and I pull her head onto my lap like she used to do a thousand years ago for me.

Go home, Sash, I say.

Her hair falls across my legs and I watch her a long time and we stay quiet.

She sits up and goes to wash her face and I give her my computer and we call her husband and we find her a flight.

THE DAY SHE leaves, my husband goes uptown to a new job and it rains, so we stay inside and the girls watch TV and draw and paint. They get in a fight over who gets to use the purple paintbrush and both of them start crying, but then the four-year-old finds another purple paintbrush and starts painting again but the two-year-old still can't stop.

Just breathe, baby, I say to her.

I try to nurse her but she pushes me away and just keeps crying, her body hot, her face bright red.

Sometimes, I say, *it helps to put your feelings other places*. I tell her that her sister puts her feelings into drawing, that I put them into running miles and miles.

She looks at me. She's hardly formed at all and trying to comprehend this thing that I just made up to calm her down. She holds her hand up to her head, then looks back at me, still crying. *But Mommy*, she says, revving up again and sounding desperate, *I can't reach my hand into my head to get the feelings out*.

8

The week after school ends, my husband's parents drive down to take the children for a week and I am weightless. Our apartment's still and quiet, empty. They take them nine hours up to northern Maine and I stand in their room every night and think about how I might drive up and bring them back.

My husband's uptown job has been extended through the week, and my friend who is quadrilingual gifts me with a week of unlimited yoga while the children are away. I go to my first class after my run early in the morning. I've installed a free-trial running app on my phone, and each morning a woman's voice tells me how many miles to run and how fast and I take comfort in her deciding all this for me in advance. The rest of the day I wander around the city. At a restaurant, I go to use the bathroom. I went yesterday and the waiters were so nice and the space so clean—the soap smelled like lemons in a way that had me touching my hands up to my face all day—and so I decide today to go again. A man sitting at the bar reading the paper, who was also, yesterday, sitting at the bar reading the paper, stops me as I walk through the main room.

I see your trick, he says.

I'm sorry? I say.

I've just showered from my run and I'm wearing a loose summer dress and a cardigan and flip-flops. I have a small tote bag filled with books.

What trick, I say.

You came here yesterday, he says. *These bathrooms are for customers. You're not.*

I'm sorry, I say, embarrassed, but also angry; also, the way he looks at and talks to me, I want to run back home and go to bed.

You can use it, he says. *But don't come back.*

I use his bathroom and wash my hands with the delicious-smelling soap and on the way out I don't look at him. I take the train back to Brooklyn and wait in a poorly air-conditioned coffee shop until the next yoga class. I get there early and lie a long time quietly on the mat.

I meet a friend who is a member at the Whitney to see a preview of a show that I can't see alone because they don't take my university IDs. I've read about this artist, and though I've never seen his work in person, I've thought about him, about what I read about his life and work, his death, for years. The first exhibit, once my friend has shown the man at the entrance proof that he's a member, is pictures, photographs in black and white of people in different parts of New York City, wearing a mask of Rimbaud's face over their own. The artist wanted to be a writer, says one of the captions. He had in common with Rimbaud his queerness, an impulse toward activism, a belief in the power and the strangeness of words when they are twisted and reconfigured to new ends.

I think of all the ways that books have failed me, all the

ways they're less than what I thought, but it's still the language that I like the best in the show. I find the colors of the paintings almost painfully off-putting; the attempts at beauty, large flowers on blue-and-green canvas, I find grotesque. But the language that he uses, its anger and its sharpness. There's an empty room with a large window that's been covered with a screen to keep most of the light out and one can sit inside the room and listen to this artist speak the angry words he's written on some of the work. He died of AIDS at thirty-seven. He lost so many of his friends. There's a fury to not just the words but the way he says them, unapologetic. I imagine, as I listen, there was spittle on his face when he was done.

That night, in bed, after we have FaceTimed with the children, after they've told us about swimming and about searching through the woods for moose; after we have gone to the cheap restaurant close to our house and had a bourbon each; after we came home and he sat down on the chair beneath our bed in our room to watch soccer and I saw him, and walked toward him, climbed on top of him, wearing a short cotton summer dress, and we had sex; after my husband's gone to sleep; after I sit up and scroll through Sasha's still unpopulated Instagram; my phone rings and it's Kayla's name across the screen.

Hello? I say.

Hi, she says, her voice flat. *You busy*?

It's 1:00 in the morning.

Not really? I say.

My husband sits up, mouthing to ask if it's the children. I shake my head and climb slowly out of bed.

You okay? I say.

Can you come here? she says. *There's been a thing.*

What kind of thing, Kayla? I say.

She lives in the Bronx, which is an hour at least from our house on the subway. We don't have a car. I can't fathom what a cab would cost.

I'm at the police station, she says. *I need someone.* She starts to cry and I reach into my closet to find jeans and a bra and T-shirt.

Tell me the address.

I tell my husband where I'm going but he's bleary, still half-sleeping. I kiss him, make sure his phone is attached to the charger, that I have an extra charger in my bag.

Keep me posted, he says, as I walk out the door.

The trains are running better than expected and I'm at the station before I told her I would be there. It's quiet, only one cop at the desk when I come in, and she motions me back.

Can I help you? asks a guy at another desk once I've entered.

I tell him Kayla's name.

He looks at me, wary. *You're not her mother*, he says.

I'm . . . I'm her teacher, I say.

She needs a legal guardian to come get her.

What happened? I say. *Is she okay?*

She needs a guardian, he says. *You have some sort of proof that you have a legal right to her?*

I don't, I say. I don't have any rights to her.

She comes out then and I go to her and hug her. Her lip is swollen. There's a bite mark on her chest.

Honey, I say.

She's not crying, hardly breathing.

Honey, I say again. *Are you okay?*

She was in an altercation with a man we now have in custody.

You didn't take her to a doctor?

She refused medical assistance, the man says.

Kayla, I say.

I'm fine, she finally says down to her feet.

Can I take her? I say. *Why would you keep her?*

If she wants to charge him with assault she has to stay.

Do you? I say. *Honey? What do you want to do?*

Kayla nods. *To stay.*

She needs a guardian, the man says. *You're not a guardian.*

I look at Kayla.

Where's your mom? I say.

She hands me her phone and I see she has eleven missed calls from her mother, texts from her also.

You didn't call her? I say.

Kayla shakes her head.

I take the phone into the front room of the precinct and I call her.

Kay? her mom says. *Baby? You okay?*

Miz Kane? I say.

I tell her who I am.

Why do you have her phone? she says. *Where's my baby?*

Miz Kane, I say, *I'm at the police precinct*. I give her the address. *Kayla got into a fight with someone*, I say. *I think. Can you come down?*

Why— then stops. She says: *I'm on my way.*

She's there within minutes, ten or twenty, head-wrapped, frantic, in jeans and T-shirt.

She runs past the front desk, straight to Kayla. She doesn't look at anyone but her.

My baby, she says. She holds her a long time, her arms around her, then straight, and she looks at her, hands on her cheeks and her face close.

She talks to the cops and they tell her what has happened.

She looks at Kayla, sharper this time. *Jesus Christ*, she says. *Are you okay?*

They hand her paperwork to sign and she signs it and she whispers to her daughter. Kayla nods, not looking at her or anywhere but down, and quiet. The cop leads Kayla, by herself, to another room.

Don't say anything until I'm there, her mother calls to her. *You're okay*, she says. *I'll be right there.*

She goes to her one more time and holds her face and whispers to her. She pulls her to her then she walks toward me.

I reach out my hand and say my name.

Kayla's mom looks at my hand and holds, then drops it. She tells me her name. *Come here*, she says.

I look past her, trying to get a glimpse of Kayla.

She'll be okay, says her mother.

She leads me further from the other cop, in front of a desk that's empty.

You have kids? she says.

I nod.

That's good, she says.

I nod again.

You want someone else trying to raise your kids?

I shake my head.

That's good too, she says.

I nod at her, not wanting to have to hear her ask me to no longer talk to Kayla. I want to still be able to talk to Kayla, but I know I won't if her mother says I can't.

Take care of yourself, she says.

I will, I tell her. *I try to.*

Take care of your kids, she says. The "your" is slightly firmer, louder, than the other words.

I nod one more time.

She looks at me long and walks back to where her daughter is.

At yoga, there's a teacher I've never had before. She's more solid than the other women, short and stocky. She wears a thin red T-shirt with white writing that pulls at her breasts and bunches overtop her ass. She has curly, light-red hair held back and wide, round legs.

This is a multilevel Vinyasa flow, she says, *which means some of your neighbors might be making modifications, so please keep your eyes off your neighbors and just follow what I say*.

She keeps saying this throughout the class, a little scolding. I always get behind and have to watch the women in front of me or behind me and I get nervous, hoping that she doesn't see me as I look.

Please take your eyes off of your neighbors, she says again, as we sit in a squat, and I think I'll never take a class with her again.

Except there is a rhythm to the class and I get inside it. We move more quickly than I'm used to and I think I'll fall or the woman behind me, whom I've seen before and who can do the headstand, will fall over laughing at the fact that I can't even touch my toes.

I sweat more than I usually do at yoga, and my back straightens and it lengthens and my stomach pulls back further to my spine and I look straight ahead.

Every day or two I get a text from Sasha, pictures of the baby. I touch my phone's screen and smile at her. I don't know how to tell her what I think, how much I hope for her and her baby, how much I wish I could be there with both of them. I send back pictures of our girls instead.

We're friends now, I think. It's different. I think maybe this time, as we try to love each other, maybe it will be more careful and less dire.

I get an email from Melissa. *Just wanted to check in to say I've been cleared*, she writes, *of whatever this whole thing was about. I wanted to thank you*, she says. She suggests we meet for dinner and I agree too quickly.

I'd love to, I say. *Tell me when and where.*

How are you? says Melissa. I see her outside. She's very thin, no longer pretty, but the structure of her face serves as a sort of palimpsest for all the ways it must have been pretty, must have been a force.

We hug although I've never hugged her. I brush my arm accidentally along her abdomen.

I don't think the food is very good here, she says. She picked the restaurant. *It's close to my apartment*, she says. *And the drinks are strong.*

I smile, not sure if I'm meant to laugh.

The host leads us to a table in a dark corner of the room. She gets a gin martini and I am grateful and I get the same and she smiles at me, showing teeth.

You've been good? she says.

She never asks about my children and I've always liked this about her. She has no children. I have heard, though she's not said this to me, that she dislikes them.

I'm so glad, I say, *that all of this is settled.*

Our drinks come and she sips hers.

She says my name. *You have no idea*, she says.

I don't know if you want to talk about it.

It's fine, she says. *It's over now.*

What happened? I say. *What did any of this have to do with you?*

David is a friend of mine, she says.

David is the man about whom the students had been talking, the man of whom I reported uncertain allegations but who now has apparently been cleared.

There are certain people, she says, *who have been out to get him. Not least because he is allied with me.*

She's a fiction writer. I've read only one of her books, and in it a woman sleeps with her sixty-five-year-old professor/mentor. She's a gorgeous writer. The book spends a good amount of time unpacking all the various ways and places they have sex. There are paragraphs describing New York, at night and early in the morning, the park, along the water, that I can still picture sometimes in my head.

There's something happening right now, she says, *a certain type of victimhood*, she says.

Our food comes.

I sip my drink and she sips hers.

It's been weaponized, she says. *Anyway*, she says, noticing that there's food before her.

What happened, though? I say. *What's happening with David?*

He was dating a student, she says.

But he's married, I want to say, and then feel strange and dumb but also angry. He's married. He has little kids.

There are all these new provincial rules because the institution is afraid, she says.

She eats her sandwich in small bites and chews it slowly.

I have a cheeseburger that I've yet to touch.

One of these hypersensitive girls thought it was not appropriate, she says.

She, this girl, she says, *not his girlfriend—she asked to be removed from his class. I told her I saw no reason for this,* she says.

She sips her drink and I press my hands against the hard wood of the table.

So she told on me, she says.

I pick up my burger and I bite.

It's still not clear to me, though, she says, *why they looped you in.*

I chew and neither of us speaks for too long for it not to be on purpose.

Yeah, I say. *Who knows?*

When I get home, my husband is in bed. Left out on the counter, meant for me to see it, is a letter telling us the owners of the building are converting it to condos. They've given us the option to purchase our apartment or to leave within the month.

I call the rich woman the next morning.

Could we get coffee? I say to her.

I have news, she says.

We've waited too long and she's pregnant. They did one round of IVF with other donor sperm she doesn't explain and it worked.

I hold briefly onto my stomach.

It's still early, she says.

Of course, I say. *Good luck.*

Were you— she starts.

Just seeing how you were.

My husband's parents keep a small farm in Maine and have very little money, but they have gotten us a rental car. We're meant to drive up to Maine to get our girls and spend the next week with them and my husband's parents. We stop in Boston to see my friend Leah, who has brand-new twins and a new house; they live up high on a hill, across the street from a small natural preserve with lots of large, dark trees in the back. They have a dog they've had since the year that they got married and she's huge now, an English bulldog, and she has bad hips and is sometimes incontinent and has to be lifted in and out of the house every hour so she doesn't pee or shit on the floor too much.

We have nothing in common, Leah and I. We met our third year of college, before we were formed enough to know who we might one day be. We like each other. We've liked each other for long enough that it feels worth it to keep being friends.

I hug her and I grab a baby from her arms when we get there. I dip my face into the top of his head and breathe him in; he squirms and is warm on my chest and I breathe out long after a week without our children. Most of the time when she's not up and moving through the house and doing something—cleaning, cooking—Leah has a baby latched on one of her breasts.

The first day and a half is all catching up and small talk. Leah's husband is extraordinarily calm and kind and my husband helps him install IKEA shelves that they bought months ago for the babies' room. They ask us about the girls and about New York, and when I say I quit the high school job Leah and her husband get quiet and look at each other.

What's the plan, then? Leah says, trying to stay neutral.

I'm not sure, I say. *I have four jobs for the fall,* I say.

I've got some things lined up, my husband says.

I want to tell her we will at least be able to care for our kids but I don't know that.

We might be without a place to live in two weeks, I don't say.

Leah puts the twins to bed and we open a third bottle of wine and sit outside looking at the trees until we all begin to fall asleep and Leah says, *We should go inside*, and we go into our separate rooms.

My husband falls asleep as soon as we get under the covers. I read for a while. I scroll through my own Instagram account, all the pictures and the videos of our daughters, years of them: babies, bigger, laughing, crawling, the last summer we were up in Maine. I go briefly to Sasha's, where there is nothing new except a single picture of the baby, red-faced, big-eyed, hairless. I like it, then plug in my phone and try to fall asleep.

I'm not sure if I've slept at all, but I hear one of the babies crying and I come out of the guest room. I feel my left breast begin to leak. Leah is there already. They've set up a small bed in the room where the babies sleep and she still stays there every night. I stand in the doorway as she goes to the crying baby. The other wakes as well and I ask if Leah wants me to get her. She nods and I scoop her up, pressing her against my chest and rocking back and forth and shushing.

Leah sits in the large stuffed rocking chair her husband's parents bought them when she was in her third trimester and they were finally not afraid to receive gifts. She unbuttons her nightshirt and places the baby to her breast. The girl I hold has settled, and I offer her my finger to gnaw until she falls back asleep in my arms.

How's it going? I say.

Leah laughs and shakes her head, still staring at the nursing baby. They're tiny; I'm sitting now and the girl feels weightless, still smaller than our girls were when they were born.

Dude, she says.

I laugh and watch her watch him: his bright-red feet, his hand held tight around her thumb.

You okay? I say.

Sort of.

The baby I hold squirms again and chirps and her cheek is hot against my chest. I offer her my knuckle, which she gnaws on, and she settles down again.

It gets better, I say.

Leah winces as the baby tries to relatch and must have pinched her. I hear him choke and sputter and I motion toward her breast.

May I? I ask.

She nods down toward the baby.

I take her breast and place my thumb into the baby's mouth until it opens fully; I place her nipple far back in his mouth and he latches on and Leah breathes out.

It's up to you, says my husband.

We've been in the car for two hours and we've just now gotten up the courage to talk about asking my parents for a loan.

What are our other options? I say.

We could move in with my parents, he says.

His parents have a one-bedroom house so far north in Maine that they're often snowed in for weeks or months.

We could do the things that people do when they don't have rich parents to call.

Our neighbor Luis is moving in with his kids upstate.

Another two are going to elder-care facilities that horrify them. The gentrifiers, the people in our building who look most like us, mostly are either buying in or finding apartments south of the park.

We could leave New York, but we'd need to rent a van and get jobs. We'd need first and last month's rent and a security deposit. We don't have a car, and our credit's shot.

We need jobs, I say to him.

I could call some of the old Lehman guys.

It's been a decade since he left that job. What was once a fancy degree, youth, and hunger is now a single year of relevant experience and creeping middle age.

What do you want, though? I say.

To pay our rent, he says. *To take care of our kids.*

Right before the reception disappears, I text my dad to ask if he's available and he texts back to say he is. I don't ask for a specific sum but explain the various parts of our dilemma as calmly and as neutrally as I can. We need enough for a deposit, three months' rent, plus we need guarantors since our credit's shot.

Don't call it a loan, though, says my father. *Don't pretend you'll be able to pay us back.*

He's put me on speaker in his car and my mom's there. The phone cuts in and out and their voices feel hollow and half-formed; I hear my mother two times mumble something to my father; I hear him say her name and tell her to calm down. They're building a new house on a new property that they just purchased. *The new construction's proving more expensive than we thought,* he says.

They ask a lot of questions, about my job and why I'm not going back to it. I think of telling them because I felt like I was dying walking into that building every morning, because I never saw my children, because I couldn't stomach watching all those kids not get what their parents had been promised they would get. I think of telling him I was making less at that job than I'll make stringing together the four jobs I've taken since then, except it still doesn't matter, except neither of these choices pays enough for us to live.

I say: *We would pay it back.*

I have the adjunct jobs, a part-time freelance gig transcribing subtitles. I've sent a résumé to the wine bar where a friend who dropped out of our grad program our third year works.

What's the plan, though? asks my mother.

I just told you.

But long term, she says. *What's the plan?*

I don't know, I tell her.

I don't know.

This can't be good for the children, says my mother. *All this stress.*

I know, I say. I do not want to start to cry then but I do.

I don't know the plan, I say. *I wish there was one,* I say. *But there's only trying to find more work. There's only hoping that it adds up to enough.*

At what point, says my mother, *is it time to cut your losses? At what point is it time to give up on this whole dream thing?*

I don't . . . I start to say but don't know what she's asking.

What dream? I ask.

9

THE TWO-YEAR-OLD IS turning three and wants a party. We can't afford to throw a party, but her sister got a party in December and she's been talking about her own since then. They've been mostly with each other the whole summer; they've started fighting more and more often; they've begun asking for their friends.

My parents decide, at the last minute, to fly up for the birthday party. They put ten thousand dollars in our bank account the week before we would have had no other options and have served as guarantors on the lease we signed for a one-bedroom apartment farther down in Brooklyn in which my husband built us another loft bed in the room off of the kitchen and our girls sleep in bunk beds that we found on Craigslist even though they're too young. Even though, every night so far since we got here, I have climbed up into bed with the four-year-old, just to be sure she doesn't fall.

I don't know how to feel about this money. I feel grateful and embarrassed. I am lucky and I'm spoiled and my kids are safe and warm and fed.

The Chilean writer's back in town for the start of the new semester and I invite her to the birthday party. I invite both of my co–homeroom teachers, and, on a whim, the twenty-four-year-old, who is the only one of the four of us who's going back to the high school next week when they start. I invite my friend who is quadrilingual and her partner, the handful of kids whose parents' contact info I have from the two- (now three-) year-old's school list. My husband bakes a cake and we go to the ninety-nine-cents store by our house and get streamers and balloons and plates and cups and napkins, tiny plastic gems that come in white net bags and that each child clutches to her as we walk around the store, that I agree to buy because it's a birthday party and they're only a dollar. We get bagels and I cut up grapes and apples and peaches, hoping none of the parents from the preschool ask if they're organic. I scrub the bathroom as I let the children watch TV and I bathe them and I dress them and I stand a while in the shower thinking what it is I'm meant to be wearing to my baby's birthday party. I put on black pants and a black shirt, then take it off and put on a long-sleeved purple dress and when the baby sees me she says, *Mommy, that's my favorite color*, and she hugs me, and I slip on flip-flops and rub the moisturizer my mom gets me every Christmas on my face.

My parents get there first and bring my sister. My mom wears a dress that's pink and green with animals all over; my father's shirt is far too crisp.

Hi, I say. I don't remember how to touch them.

Our girls come running out to greet them. They lift them up and hold them, kiss them. I let them play together as my husband and I continue to set up.

Three years old, I hear my mother say. *I remember when your mom was three.*

Our girls ask her a thousand questions, and I hear her laugh, and I can see her smiling though I can't see them.

She was wild, she says. *Always naked. She learned to swim at two and would have spent all day in the ocean if she could.*

The buzzer starts to buzz and people trudge up the three flights of stairs to our new place. *There are too many people*, says my husband. We have the single window unit in the window, but we are all in the same small room next to the kitchen, and the stove's still on from the cake that's baking and all of us begin to sweat and the kids run back and forth between the kitchen and their room.

I watch my mom the whole time. She kneels down to talk to all the children. Her arms are very thin, her shoulders thick with freckles, and she gestures a lot when she talks, like me. The Chilean writer comes in, and I hug her. I stand in the hall with her a minute and she holds my elbow and I think that I might tell her all of what the last six weeks have been like, but instead I hug her again and she leads me back inside. My co–homeroom teacher has driven from New Jersey, where she is now in med school. The twenty-four-year-old sits on one of the small IKEA chairs and eats from a bowl of popcorn, though he's six feet three at least and it looks like, any moment, the chair might break beneath him; he hunches over, and I try to offer him a beer.

Gifts pile up on the table next to the food and the cake and the water pitcher that we've set out. I've set up a roll of butcher paper on the floor of the girls' room with paints that, I hope, I tell the other parents, are mostly washable. The kids paint the paper, then each other. The parents all go back out into the kitchen to get more wine and beer. My mom takes pictures and my dad sits on the couch with my other younger co–homeroom teacher and asks her about grad school. He holds his ankle on his knee and I watch him as she smiles as he asks her another question and she answers and he smiles back.

We have forgotten candles. The Chilean writer takes my keys and walks the two blocks to the bodega and comes back with candles that turn out to be trick candles and the two-year-old blows six times before the fire's finally out. Everybody laughs and, though I worry that she'll cry, the now three-year-old thinks the fire's magic and she claps and when the candles are all out she looks sad. I give her all of them piled on a plate so she can lick the frosting off and she seems better. We serve the cake and everybody tells me it's delicious and I have to keep saying, *It wasn't me, it was my husband*, and they all look at him, then me again, and I shake my head and he smiles from the kitchen with the four-year-old up in his arms.

Someone gets paint on the girls' sheets and someone else pees in the kitchen. My mother posts a whole album of pictures on the internet in real time, and the twenty-four-year-old leaves early and as he leaves he shakes my hand. I hug my co–homeroom teachers as I walk them to their cars and tell them not to forget to call me. The Chilean writer sits on our couch and makes my husband laugh. My dad starts cleaning up the girls' room by himself and I tell him to stop but he doesn't listen. My sister's holding someone's baby but I don't know whose.

ELIZABETH, SAYS MY mother. She's the only person in the world who can say my name and make it mean; I hear her close to me and I turn.

The apartment's mostly empty. I can hear my husband and the Chilean writer still talking in the other room.

I think of all the ways this isn't what it should be, that I'm not. That there is a corner of the bathroom where grout and mold have become one and even though I scrubbed at it for half an hour, she would have known how to make it better and I don't. The floor of the girls' room is covered in paint and toys and Duplos. There's half a piece of cake smeared into the four-year-old's pillow.

It was nice, says my mother.

I shrug, looking down at my feet and all the Duplos.

I go to pick one up and throw it in a bin. She leans over behind me and hands me a small pink My Little Pony, another Duplo. I pick up a doll's dress, a stuffed dog, a stuffed horse, three tiny plastic dinosaurs. I listen as she throws magnet tiles into a bin. I try to scrape the frosting off the four-year-old's pillow with my fingers. Once, when I was up in my room crying—when I was fourteen and often up in my room crying, and she often stayed downstairs and made the dinner and talked to my dad and sister and pretended that I wasn't there—but once, she climbed up the stairs and held me on her lap though I was bigger than her and she rocked me back and forth and held my hand.

We both stand up straight, the floor mostly cleared, though I can see toys still underneath the kids' beds. My girls run by and I think that she might touch me but she doesn't. The baby comes up to grab hold of my leg and her sister barrels in behind. My mom watches them and me, I think, though I don't turn toward her.

She says: *They're so beautiful, Elizabeth.*

The baby starts to cry because her sister is on top of her and holding on to her too tightly and I pick her up and then her sister starts to cry because her sister's being held and she wants to be held too and also her sister is the only one who got any presents and birthdays aren't fair and someone stole the frosting off her cake and now there isn't any more. I lean over to lift her too, but my mom gets to her first and holds her in her arms.

I turn toward her and I smile. The four-year-old grabs hold of my mom's face and presses her cheeks inward. The now three-year-old leans her hot cheek against mine and I say, *Thanks.*

ACKNOWLEDGMENTS

To Kerry Cullen and Sarah Bowlin, who believed so surely in this thing.

To early readers, talkers, thinkers: Miranda Popkey, Marcy Dermansky, Lindsay Hatton, Adrienne Celt, Lucas Knipscher, Bryant Musgrove, Robin Wasserman, Rebecca Taylor, and always and especially, Rumaan Alam.

To writer dinner ladies: Elena Megalos, Eliza Schraeder, Yurina Ko, Sanaë Lemoine.

To Karen and Sam Steger, Cristina de la Vega and Kenny Strong, Kayleen Hartman and Emily Bender, and families born into, married, and chosen.

To Zipporah Wiseman, for that conversation in the car about what to make and why.

To all my students past and present, for your investment, excitement, generosity, and care.

To Peter, Isabel, and Luisa, for everything you are.

ABOUT THE AUTHOR

LYNN STEGER STRONG's first novel, *Hold Still*, was released by Liveright/W. W. Norton in 2016. Her nonfiction has been published in *The Paris Review*, *The Cut*, *Guernica*, the *Los Angeles Review of Books*, Elle.com, Catapult, Literary Hub, and elsewhere. She teaches both fiction and nonfiction writing.